THE·PRIVATE·RICH
A FAMILY ALBUM

THE·PRIVATE·RICH

·A FAMILY ALBUM·

Stories by Peter Rand
Photographs edited by Elizabeth Bird

Crown Publishers, Inc., New York

For Bliss and Jamie   —P. R.

For Lance and Lola   —E. B.

Published by Crown Publishers, Inc., One Park Avenue, New York, New York 10016 and simultaneously in Canada By General Publishing Company Limited Manufactured in the United States of America

Library of Congress Cataloging in Publication Data
Rand, Peter, 1940–
The private rich.
1. Wealth—Fiction. I. Bird, Elizabeth.
II. Title.
PS3568.A48P7   1984   813'.54   84–14273

ISBN: 0-517-55449-6
10 9 8 7 6 5 4 3 2 1
First Edition

Design by Dennis Lo

Any resemblance between the characters in the written text of *The Private Rich* and people, living or dead, is purely coincidental. The photographs, furthermore, are entirely independent of the written text and do not represent the characters therein. The written text and photographs merely complement each other in a manner intended to capture, poetically speaking, the spirit of a vanishing social milieu.

Contents

Foreword

The family album you hold open before you is a guided tour of the secluded life of upper-class Americans during the better part of the twentieth century. Photographs of this generic family have been collected from various sources around the country; some were carefully selected from archives and museums, others are found photographs or snapshots taken from family albums. The stories, legends about the rich, do not depict any of the individuals who appear in the photographs.

This guided tour has been carefully planned. It begins with a group of exterior photographs that establish a sense of order and place peculiar to the private rich. From the outdoors you will be guided across grounds into the rooms where the rich privately enact the *opéra comique* described in the stories. In the photographic sections that follow you will travel to parts of the world they frequent, meet them at play, encounter their ancestors, and experience the style and mood of the privileged life. By the end you will know these people in their aboriginal settings.

As your tour guide and narrator, I will entertain you along the way with stories from my personal stock. These stories reveal a layer of reality beneath the surface of the photographs. Thus, the tale betrays the photograph even as the photograph captures the real image of this fabulous world. Look at the photos. Read the stories. Now browse among the pictures once again. What do you see?

H. Bradfield Marquand

Cousins

Anson, the black sheep of the family, was one day older than Bronson, his first cousin. Bronson, however, was bigger. Bronson was structured like a Neanderthal. His head grew forward out of a long sloping trunk. He was a powerful athlete. But he was also slower than Anson. It took him a while to think things through. Anson very often didn't bother to do this at all. He was indifferent to most mental exercises. He saw no reason to bother figuring out answers to problems. He had fallen heir, by an accident of timing, to the name of the great family progenitor and this was enough. Bronson, a day later, was named after someone his father had known in college.

They both lived in New York. Bronson's father was a judge on the United States Court of Appeals. Anson, whose father was the family buccaneer, lived with his mother, Flo Havershaw, a famous beauty of her day who had performed on the London stage during the reign of Edward the Seventh. Florence, for that was how she preferred to be called, conducted a morning salon at her house on Fifth Avenue. Here Anson picked up the latest inside dope about the beau monde. He was sophisticated at an early age. He traveled all over Europe with his mother and as a child was even a little world weary. He was diffident and easily bored.

Bronson never passed judgment on Anson. He held his cousin in awe. When they summered together in childhood Anson entranced Bronson with tales about the antic rich. Also, he brightened Bronson's soul without warning. Once, in Scotland, he told Bronson—they were twelve at the time—"I'm going off now. So long. You won't see me again for the time being."

"But wait a minute," Bronson said. "We're out in the middle of nowhere."

"I doubt if that's of much importance," Anson replied. He got to his feet. "Bronny," he said and snickered. He departed, ascending the deep hollow between two hills. He disappeared up into the shadow of the hollow. Bronson didn't know whether he was hiding up there or whether he really had disappeared. He waited for Anson until the late evening air cooled to a pure green-blue color, and he began to get cold.

"All right, Anson," Bronson called up into the evening shadows. "You

1

win. I'm going home. But we'll see who's ahead in the morning." He went back to the castle where they were staying with his grandmother and grandfather, his mother's parents, the earl and countess of Something and Something Else. He told them that Anson had decided to make an all-night trek. Actually, Anson had altogether disappeared and a search party was sent out to find him. He was discovered days later. He was staying at a castle that was now a golf resort on the west coast, famous for serving the best pastry in the United Kingdom. He'd hoodwinked the management by dropping the names and addresses of some hotel regulars from the Continent, in French, which he knew to perfection. The furious earl had to settle the bill out of his own pocket, and Bronson didn't see Anson again until, months later, they showed up at the same dancing class.

Bronson could never explain Anson to anyone's satisfaction. He was sometimes consulted about Anson by his elders, who treated Bronson like a junior partner, but his interpretations were often unacceptable. He couldn't alter the earl's opinion of Anson, for instance.

For six years Anson and Bronson attended the same New England boarding school. The other boys took immediate objection to Anson and would have nothing to do with him. On this matter alone they ignored Bronson, who was perhaps the best-liked boy in their class. Bronson agonized for his cousin in silence. Privately he tried, unsuccessfully, to change Anson's way of talking. He advised him never to speak of his father, who had achieved international notoriety when a wire service reporter saw him hurl a platter of *tête de veau* across the dining room at the Café de la Paix. Anson maintained that his father had been attempting to get the attention of a waiter, not a reporter.

"Too many people hate him," Bronson told Anson. "He's a swaggart and something of a fraud."

"Who calls him a swaggart?" Anson demanded to know.

"My father, for one," said Bronson somberly.

"Your father is a horse's neck," Anson replied, in French, which Bronson understood but couldn't speak.

"He's older than your father," Bronson said slowly. "Anyway, I'd play it down."

Bronson was astonished to find that Anson did not reciprocate his discretion. One Saturday afternoon he overheard his cousin gossiping with some younger boys beneath the window of the school library where Bronson was laboring to translate one of Cicero's orations into acceptable English.

"Bronny's a soft touch," Anson said clearly, almost as though he knew that Bronson would hear him. The rest was inaudible. Afterward, Bronson sorrowed over the estrangement this created between them.

Anson was a prisoner of war at boarding school. This, at any rate, was how he behaved. He was often in solitary confinement working off black marks or making up homework. Otherwise he seemed to have more time on his hands than he knew what to do with, although much of it he was able to idle away with younger boys, whom he beguiled with stories about his exploits in Europe. Finally, the headmaster gave up on Anson. He called Bronson into his study. He told Bronson that Anson would have to go. This was better all around, he said. Anson just wasn't the kind of boy the school was intended to help. "Look here," he said. He became suddenly impassioned. "He simply doesn't do a lick of work."

"He's good at French," Bronson said.

The Deacon, as the headmaster was known, begged to differ on that point.

"He can't do French," the Deacon said. "He doesn't even know the *passé simple.*" He craned forward with incredulity. "Even *I* know the *passé simple,*" he confided. "No. It won't do. I've written to his mama." The Deacon's eyes traveled around over his desk top while he touched all the papers on his desk, like a blind person. "Ah," he said. "Here it is." He held up a sheet of stationery covered with his own handwriting. "It explains everything," he said. "Of course I've written to her about Anson before, but it hasn't done much good. She'll understand, I think, that we've tried to do our level best. Be kind and soften the blow for old Anson, and smooth it out with his mother if you possibly can."

Bronson did nothing of the kind. He went to a ranch in Wyoming that summer and never gave Anson a thought.

He was amazed to find Anson aboard the school train at Grand Central in September with all the other New York boys. He nevertheless kept his counsel. Anson was, as usual, diffident and a little sallow. Perhaps the Deacon had changed his mind, although this seemed unlikely. Back at school Bronson stood well behind Anson when they lined up to shake the hand of the headmaster, who by tradition stood outside the dining room with his wife beside him and greeted each new and returning boy by name. When Anson stepped before him there was a stunning silence. The Deacon reddened briefly. He grasped Anson's shoulder.

"Did you ever get my letter?" he shouted.

Anson replied that he had not.

"Then I'd like to see you later in my study," the Deacon announced abruptly, not wanting to hold up the line and create an impasse.

For years Bronson never knew exactly what had happened. Anson remained at school. Each year the scene repeated itself. Annually he returned on the train from New York with everyone else, stood in line, and stepped up before the headmaster, who reddened and then, as if they had worked out a comic routine, always shouted, "Did you ever get my letter?"

Anson always replied that he had not.

"Then I'd like to see you later in my study," the Deacon proceeded to say, on cue.

It was always too complicated to expel someone in the fall, which Anson and the Deacon both knew. Anson never actually earned a diploma, however. After graduation he went to a tutoring school in Munich. He got to know the German and Austrian nobility and stayed on in Europe, reputedly hunting boar in the forests of Hungary, skiing in Austria, and so forth. He split the remains of his father's fortune with his brother, Horace. This had been drastically reduced with the advent of the U.S. income tax, but it was nothing to sneeze at. The patrimony hit Anson while he was still trying to make up his mind about a profession, and he forthwith abandoned any formal plans of that kind. Instead, he lived a life of legendary extravagance in Depression-era Europe.

Anson was famous among a clique of young men who had known him at school. They had ridiculed him then, but now, from afar, they followed his career with fascination. He was a fixture on the fastest European social circuit. He always paid his way. He owned a Delahaye. He ordered his shirts from Charvet. His suits were made to order by a tailor in Zurich. He chartered a yacht one summer, invited assorted nobles to join him on board, and chased a flotilla of British yachts around the Mediterranean, hitting all the best parties on the French Riviera.

That September it was announced that Anson was engaged to marry the daughter of the pretender to the throne of a small European empire. The marriage took place in Vienna the following spring on the very day of Bronson's wedding in Newport, Rhode Island. Anson's wedding made the front page of the *New York Times* Sunday edition. Bronson's wedding, which was not an affair of state, made the front page of the Society Section of the same edition.

Anson's mother died. Bronson, an executor, was appointed the task of sifting through her papers in search of assets. Her papers had been locked up in trunks in the basement of her Fifth Avenue house. Bronson had them hauled upstairs and lined up along the bare parquet floor of the ballroom. The late Florence Havershaw had died deeply in debt and her house was due to be auctioned to pay off the bills. Bronson found many of these, unopened, in the moldering steamer trunks. Anson's mother had never opened her mail. Bronson confronted heaps of still fresh, thickly packed envelopes bearing the return addresses of poets, statesmen, foreign diplomats, opera singers, and popular violinists from a vanished age. He could recall how his aunt sat straight up in her bed in a quilted, pale pink bed jacket and conducted her morning salon. She was ravishing, to his recollection, with beautiful cheekbones. She was impatient of interruption and commanded the attention of her audience with piercing looks. Now here were the headmaster's letters, along with the rest of her unopened mail.

Anson brought his wife and two children back to the States after the war. It was a new beginning. He was a fresh, interesting arrival on the East Coast scene, especially in the company of his wife, who was known as the Infanta. Everybody wanted to meet the Infanta.

Anson now hoisted the right side of his upper lip when he talked. His hair, once fine and touched with gold, had grown lank, so that his scalp showed through in places. He wore blue-tinted spectacles. He wore a moustache, which added a raffish, aristocratic touch to his raised upper lip.

The Infanta was somewhat disappointing. She kept her passionate pride to herself. She was short, dark-haired, and intensely religious. She looked at the world with penetrating black eyes. She was also very correct, as she had been taught to be in the presence of all people. Anson took her around to New York dinner parties and handled her like a priceless, but negotiable, altarpiece. He spoke to her in French, although he spoke about her in English, and then translated what he had said into French for her benefit, although she spoke English and understood it well enough. Anson ensconced her in Philadelphia while she was still a novelty and commuted down there to see her on weekends.

Bronson invited Anson to join the Camelot Club. This was not an especially difficult offer for him to make because he was president of it. Besides, Anson was already a member of the Jockey Club of Madrid, which maintained at that time a reciprocal arrangement with the Camelot Club. Anson pointed this out to Bronson. Bronson gave him the point. But you do see, don't you, he said, it's all very well to sit at the Round Table on the Jockey, but you can't have Knight's Privileges unless you actually belong. Anson didn't know what Knight's Privileges were but he gave Bronson the go-ahead and Bronson went after the necessary signatures. He jumped Anson over other applicants on the waiting list and got him knighted in a matter of weeks.

Anson became a club fixture. It was a little disturbing to Bronson that he used it as much as he did. He always seemed to be in the taproom when Bronson stepped in for a drink before lunch, or dinner, for a confidential chat with someone from the bank. The taproom was quite intimate. Anson usually stood at the bar, one gray suede shoe on the footrail, drinking the Club Special. He always lofted Bronson an ostentatious greeting, which was hale of him, Bronson thought, if not exactly discreet. Sometimes he would have preferred to slip in unnoticed. Anson, however, could see Bronson's entrance reflected in the mirror behind the bar.

Turning, he'd say, "Hello, Bronny."

"Anson," Bronson would murmur, frowning.

Soon Anson was the hub of an ongoing cocktail party in the taproom. Bronson had not foreseen this development. A man who called himself the Baron Gunder Von Gieseling was Anson's constant guest and side-kick. The baron was just about intolerable. He chain-smoked vile Russian Sobranies. He was detestable looking with a pallor like baked clay. He had a gregarious baritone laugh that exposed his yellow canines and was accompanied by a gaze of ruthless intensity. He may not have had a fixed address. It was said at the club that he shaved every morning in the men's room of the Plaza Hotel.

Anson and the baron were in some kind of business together, which took them to board meetings in Toronto. Otherwise they did all their business in the taproom. Anson introduced the baron to club members as the executive vice-president in charge of sales of his Canadian investment company. Bronson tried to get in and out of the taproom without ever speaking to either of them. He'd catch a glimpse of them after lunch from out in the hallway when he passed the taproom on his way back to work. The taproom was often thick now with the haze of Sobranies. He wondered if Anson and the baron ever ate.

They almost became an issue at one of the monthly Round Table meetings, over which Bronson presided. Club members were not supposed to solicit business in the taproom. Also, one old member wanted to ban foreign cigarettes from the taproom. Bronson managed to table these matters, however, and then, just at its most intense, the carnival left town. One day Anson and the baron were gone. Anson had defaulted on his club bills and left no forwarding address. Bronson found out about this before anyone else at the club. He told the club manager that he would cover Anson's whopping account. He planned to reimburse himself from the family trustees, a firm of lawyers with an alliterative name that handled Anson's inheritance.

All that remained of Anson's fortune, however, was what is known as a spendthrift trust, an unbreakable trust fund devised to prevent people like Anson from squandering their principal. The income from this went to the Infanta down in Philadelphia. Anson had used the bulk of his patrimony, or what remained of it after his European extravaganza, to try to inflate the stock value of a nonexistent Canadian mining company he'd set up in cahoots with the baron. The scheme had collapsed and Anson had gone into hiding in upstate New York.

He was back in the taproom after a suitable absence. Bronson was aghast.

"Anson, good God, I thought you'd defected to Denmark," he said with a laugh. This was unintended. In his mind he had taken a sober tone when speaking to Anson. He meant to follow his opening with an urgent chat about Anson's finances. Anson, however, forestalled him. He drew a long envelope from the inside pocket of his blazer and handed it to Bronson.

"This is what I owe you, minus the interest," he said. "Better count it."

Bronson, in spite of himself, counted out the cash. This took time because the bills were fresh from the mint and adhered to one another. Anson, in the meantime, ordered a pair of Club Specials. Bronson saw when he glanced at the mirror a green-tinged Anson with a ragged moustache.

"At the moment I'm in the pizza business," he said to Bronson, "trying to recoup our investors' money. Awful strain on Carlotta. But"—he raised his glass to Bronson—"I hope this won't affect your reputation at the Round Table."

"Of course not," Bronson replied. "Good heavens. The pizza business." He managed a laugh. Pizza. Ovens. Equipment. You have to have money for that. "No, no, quite the ticket," he said and looked Anson in the eye. It made him think of the Deacon. Anson's eye, as indeed the Deacon must have noted, was ice blue. Very far north. His own eye he knew to be brown.

Anson's bad checks did him in, finally. These began to bounce like tennis balls at the Camelot Club. Some of them were written late at night to pay for his drinks with the baron, who had quietly started showing up again in the evenings. Others, as the bookkeeper put it at a special meeting of club officers, were just plain bad. "He is using the club as a source of personal revenue," the bookkeeper said.

Bronson requested, and was granted, permission to leave the room while the board took a vote. The officers agreed unanimously to deliver a warning to Anson. This was the procedure. A letter was handed to

Anson at the bar the following evening by the hall porter. Anson fitted the sealed envelope into the left-hand inside pocket of his blazer. It is not known whether he ever opened it. The following week a battery of checks came back from a bank in Ohio. He was then expelled from the club.

Bronson expelled him. He had been obliged in his official capacity to call Anson into his office. He chose to see him in his office at the bank instead of at the club. He had, he explained to Anson, absented himself from the final vote. It was not his personal decision. He would not put himself in a position to pass judgment on Anson. Anson took the news with his usual composure. He spoke to Bronson from the door as he was leaving.

"I understand, Bronny," he said. "I knew you'd take it out on me, from the day I upstaged you in the *Times.*" He said it in French.

Bronson, as it happened, was the one who discovered him two weeks later having drinks at the bar. He'd spotted the baron first. The baron was sprawled on a barstool with his head propped on the palm of his hand listening while Anson told a story. Anson stood with his back to the door. The baron snatched a glance at Bronson but continued to listen to Anson without any change of expression. People in the taproom fell silent as they became aware of Bronson, who loomed soundlessly between the threshold and the bar, head forward on his neck, staring at Anson.

"Which was one for my poor old papa," they all heard Anson say. This time the baron did not laugh. Anson lifted his brandy snifter and drained it. Then he turned his head and shoulders in the direction of Bronson.

"All right, Anson," Bronson said softly, and in a rising voice he called out, as though into the hollow between two smooth hills, into the pure, clear northern air of the evening, to Anson, his cousin, departed: "It's all right, whatever you do is all right, Anson, as far as I'm concerned. You win. I'm going home. But we'll see who's ahead in the morning."

That was all. Embarrassed, he turned and strode out of the room.

The very next day the Camelot Club canceled its reciprocal arrangement with the Jockey Club of Madrid.

Pirates

In Cuernavaca, our mother played duets on the piano every Tuesday morning with a woman named Frederika Russell. Mrs. Russell was an inscrutable heiress from Long Island. She often looked quite cross, although I believe she was simply nearsighted. She parted her fine, thin hair in the middle and wore it in tight curls that revealed her long, graceful neck to advantage. She was a fairly intelligent woman, although not college educated. She appeared on the scene with a stylish second act. Her first husband, it was understood, had been a Coldstream Guard who now lived on a remittance somewhere in Africa. Mrs. Russell was found to be living behind the cool white walls of a Spanish colonial residence. It was only dimly possible to imagine how she occupied herself when she was inside it. The walls also contained extensive grounds, including a wide green lawn where her sons by Mr. Russell could practice playing polo. Franco Russell, her husband, was an American, but he possessed some essential nobility. He had been in a Broadway play. He drove a two-door maroon Cadillac convertible with a bone white steering wheel. He always drove with the top down, so that his white hair lifted in the rush of open air like a plume. He had a bravura technique of actually turning to face us in the back seat, to talk, while he was driving. I cannot remember anything he said. I only recall his face and his thick lenses and the tortoiseshell frames of his glasses. He would have worn an ascot and a hound's-tooth jacket.

The Russell boys were wonderful. They had blond, flaxen hair. Their mother, when she smiled, had brilliant teeth and elegant dimples, and the Russell boys all inherited this winning, Germanic smile. Their father taught them to ride, and when they were still very young he took them down to Acapulco on weekends and made them repeatedly dive from the high cliffs into shallow water like the local Mexican boys until they were without fear. They grew up to be superb athletes. Each one of the Russell boys learned to speak French and Spanish as well as English, which they spoke in an unmistakably upper-class British accent. This was undoubtedly the result of Mrs. Russell's influence. She employed British governesses to look after them. They were bright and talented, decent, good-hearted boys. Mr. and Mrs. Russell were tall and handsome, and altogether the Russells, who were extremely photogenic, made a model family photograph.

19

In truth there was some family static. One rarely saw Mr. and Mrs. Russell together. Why wasn't Mrs. Russell warming up the front seat when we went to Mexico City for the day? Where was Mr. Russell when we went to the big family birthday barbecue at the Rincón? Mrs. Russell was there. She wore a tweed skirt, a soft wool sweater, and pearls. Her shoes were low-heeled English leather pumps. She would have worn dark glasses. Years later we learned that Russell had been on the prowl. He had taken our mother to Taxco, on a picnic, in the Parque de Artillería. The picnic, planned by Mr. Russell, had originally included his wife, but when the time came for the outing Russell showed up solo in his convertible and announced that Mrs. Russell was indisposed, which made our mother quite cross, although she agreed to go along, since it would have created some unpleasantness had she decided not to, and besides, Russell had packed an elaborate hamper. He trotted up and down the parade ground in his bathing suit within sight of our mother, she thought, to show off his World War I battle scars, which she did not find in the least bit attractive. Mr. Russell drove all the way back to Cuernavaca at eighty miles an hour. Eventually he packed up and left town with a Swedish masseuse.

The duets continued. Mrs. Russell seemed a little more nearsighted. She appears to have been rather stoic. She was no longer radiant but her smile still conveyed sudden warmth. Our mother, I believe, was one of her closer friends at this time. They belonged to a small set of grass widows with growing children. One Saturday afternoon Mrs. Russell, whose economic situation never appeared to waver, married a Dane. Our mother was Mrs. Russell's maid of honor. The Dane was not entirely bald but close to it. He was black from being in the sun, like a pirate bosun. He wore dark gray pinstripe suits, conservative paisley neckties, and darkly polished cordovan shoes. He was certainly in luck. He and Mrs. Russell immediately flew to New York from Mexico City and sailed to England first class on one of the better ocean liners that plied the Atlantic in those days and on which, as it happened, Mrs. Russell met the man who subsequently became her fourth husband. While they were abroad the Dane went to Glasgow and put in an order for a yacht. The Danes invented the yacht, once upon a time, in order to chase pirates, but I do not know exactly to what purpose this Dane proposed to put his yacht.

After a time the newlyweds returned from Europe to await the construction of the yacht. The Russells had made a transition in the meantime from one house to another. It was a sunnier house, not quite so colonial. It was on a tight corner behind cactus plants. Not too many trees. Not too many upstairs rooms. Not too many bathrooms. Beautiful view of the distant volcanoes. The Dane barked commands at the boys. He really took over. He put signs up all over the house. Don't Wipe Your Dirty Shoes on the Stairs. Don't Walk Through the House with Dirty Shoes on. Take Off Your Dirty Shoes. The house was just crammed with antique furniture.

The Dane entered his filly in a mighty fast race. Every so often they showed up at our house. Every so often the Dane went to Scotland to check on the progress of the yacht. Once, I recall, the Dane came by himself in the late morning to call for his wife after her session at the piano with our mother. It's possible that at this time our house was off limits to most people, owing to the presence therein of a bullfighter who was lying low for various reasons. In any case the Dane parked in the shade of a hedge on the uphill shoulder of the street outside our villa. It was where a chauffeur would have parked. He was driving a spit-polished gray Chrysler New Yorker convertible with red leather upholstery. He waited outside on the street in a businesslike way. I guess Mrs. Russell was supposed to meet him out there at some previously agreed upon time. That summer one of my brothers went to Durango with the Russell boys to spend a few weeks on a guest ranch with the Dane and their mother. "Uncle Jorge," as they called the Dane, drove most of the way dressed, I have always imagined, in a gray pinstripe suit, and he managed to make this drive, which was ordinarily a three-day trip, in a solid two days, with stops along the route at some smart Mexican caravansaries.

Our mother, meanwhile, had gone ahead and married the matador. For complicated financial reasons they had been compelled to conceal their marriage for a while. Later, they returned from a trip to Lake Pátzcuaro and held a wedding reception on a hot Saturday afternoon, and neither the Dane nor Mrs. Russell attended. Later Mrs. Russell gave our mother a silver charm bracelet made in Taxco as a wedding present. Then she announced over lunch at the country club that the duets would have to be discontinued. This was on orders from the Dane. He forbade them, she said, on the grounds that our mother had married beneath her social class. Now, I ask you, is this the mind of the heiress at work? Or was it the pirate? To conclude, the final departure of the Dane was called for after he had installed, in a downstairs guest room, his lover, a British sea captain, a genuine sea captain, who wore a real sea captain's uniform, including a white captain's shirt with short sleeves that I believe were embroidered with little blue anchors, although I am not absolutely sure about that. He had a gingery beard. He had been signed on as captain of the yacht, but whether he ever got to sail it I do not know.

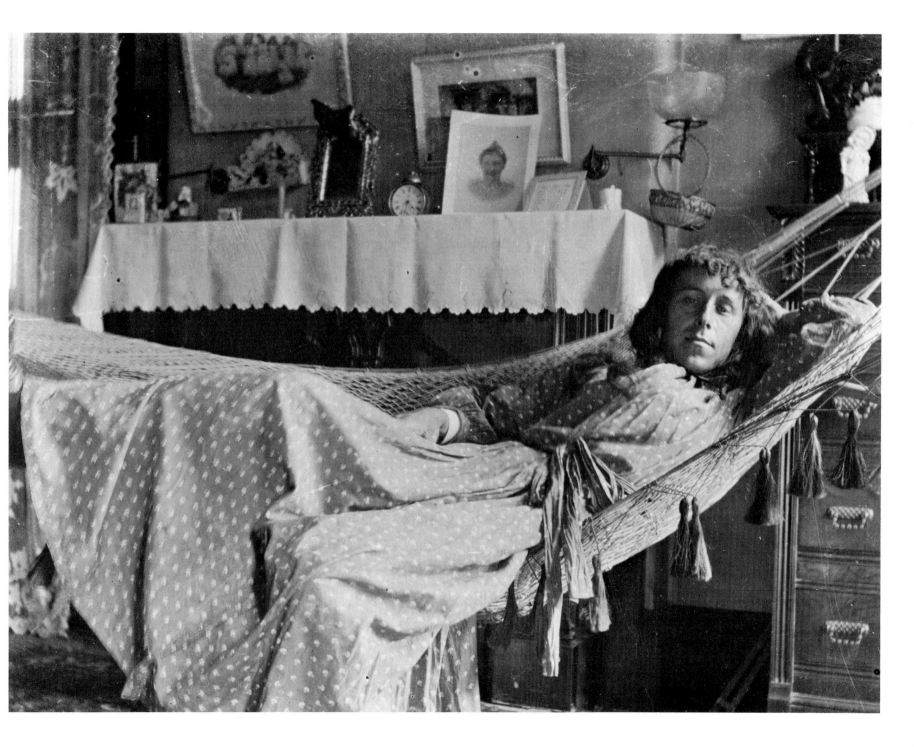

A Grandson of the Golden West

Harding Thorston our father always called *Mister* Thorston. He had the utmost regard, always, for Mr. Thorston, who, he said, had one of the fastest minds in the West. Mr. Thorston qualified as a native son of the Golden West because he belonged to a family that had settled in California before the gold rush. He had inherited a bank and when still a young man had made use of it to assemble a small financial empire. He had devoted himself in the years that followed mainly to matters concerning his family, which he called Big Top. Mr. Thorston was extremely reticent. He had said much over the years, one suspects, but by the time our father came to know him he spoke advisedly.

He spoke to our father. He spoke to his wife. He sometimes spoke at large to his family when it was gathered in the living room of the Thorstons' house. On these occasions he was present in a comfortable low armchair, the armrests of which he liked to massage with his fingertips. His massive, bald head he reclined against the back of the armchair at a slight angle. Mr. Thorston had an immobile, stoic face. Sometimes he looked almost asleep in his chair. Had he been drinking? This, in his opinion, strictly personal matter was a source of constant speculation to his whole family. He had consumed enormous amounts of liquor in his lifetime, that much was known. His alcoholic exploits were legendary. He was much admired for once having escaped from a drying-out place by sliding down a drainpipe while the director was engaged in conversation with Mrs. Thorston during a tour of the upstairs rooms. In recent years, however, only once had he been seen to lurch in the presence of guests, who were instantly reminded by Mrs. Thorston that her husband suffered from an old inner-ear disturbance he had acquired as an aide to General Pershing in the war with Mexico. Mr. Thorston dressed with flair, which was expressed by the dashing silk handkerchief he tucked in his breast pocket and by the hue of his bow tie.

The Thorston daughters and their mother talked nonstop. They had tremendous exuberance. Daughter one was high strung and could be seen turning her head this way and that, snapping her hair, like someone watching a crazy high-speed tennis match. What wonderful blue eyes she had. They were Mr. Thorston's eyes. She had his ruddy, high cheekbones and the same solid construction. She was irrepressible. His next daughter had made an interesting marriage and lived elsewhere and only came back on visits. When present, her magnificent voice dominated the room, although, as her father had on more than one occasion pointed out, she was up against the mighty gun. Mrs. Thorston commanded her end of the room in something like repose, although she argued her case ferociously. She dressed for travel. She wore immaculately tailored suits and city shoes. She looked as though she had just arrived from the airport, and often she had. She was a restless woman. She was prepared to depart at a moment's notice for New York, or Zurich, where she was an ongoing patient of Dr. Jung. The youngest daughter was Thorston's kitten. She looked most like her mother, with the same smooth brown skin her mother had possessed as a young woman, and green eyes. She had a foggy, silvery voice. She was the mother of Mason.

Mason was not unrelated, temperamentally, to the women of his family. He was a visible manifestation of how they often felt, but he was without their sense of play. He could be a sweet child, but he ran through good moods quickly and then he'd bash some other child's head with a Coke bottle and the ambulance would have to be summoned. Mason ruined many afternoons this way. His father had departed the scene shortly after his birth, never to return, and although his mother's men friends tried to punish him, his violent temper knew no limits. He overrode the men and drove them from his mother's house.

When he was about six his grandmother arranged to send Mason away to a ranch school. There, it was hoped, his fury would expend itself on the range, but after a year he was expelled with another inmate for attempting to burn down a bunkhouse. His grandmother immediately placed him in a new school, one that specialized in pack trips. By the time he was thrown out of that one his mother had remarried. Mason was not welcome in her new household and he moved in with Mr. and Mrs. Thorston instead. Mrs. Thorston was always willing to go a few rounds with Mason. Nobody else electrified Mrs. Thorston the way Mason did. She was stimulated by the novelty of his violence, although she couldn't have him in the house for long.

Mr. Thorston remained impervious to Mason. He almost never spoke to the boy. He did not like to have to look into Mason's troubled eyes.

He was prepared to speak about him. Once he came back from a long visit to the linen closet and offered to drive Mason down into the Sierra Madre. "Harding, good heavens, what an appalling idea," exclaimed Mrs. Thorston ferociously from her end of the room and scotched that plan. Instead, she delivered Mason to a school in Switzerland, which gave her a chance to visit Jung. After that Mr. Thorston did not see his wife for a long time, although she telephoned him at odd hours during the day and night to check in with Big Top and give him the lowdown on the Jung Institute, which was another circus.

Mason supposedly was at his best when he traveled on trains. He spent his holidays racing through Europe on trains, always first class. Mrs. Thorston would fly from Zurich to Paris, and then from Paris to Venice, and so on, in order to meet one train and send the boy off on another, although not infrequently she called upon family friends in various European cities to perform this task on her behalf. The boy, though he was not predictable as an overnight guest in other people's houses, was nevertheless manageable between trains. On trains, traveling by himself, he had never been known to cause trouble. Train travel should by all means be encouraged, Jung told Mrs. Thorston, who often quoted him.

Mason was confined for some years to a stone fortress on the shore of a Swiss lake. At fourteen he was placed in a coeducational boarding school in the Ojai Valley attended by the children of movie stars. Now, on his vacations, Mason rode the American rails. One summer Mason journeyed by train around the Southwest, being met at various stops by friends and relatives who had been organized into committees of welcome by Mrs. Thorston. She had decided that Mason would have a stimulating summer if he knew that people were waiting down the line to cheer him on, as Mr. Thorston observed, like the fans of Pancho Villa. Mr. Thorston lunched with Mason, between trains, at the Pasadena train station. The boy did not look well. He scowled like someone with bad digestion. He reserved special scorn for American railroad food. He insisted on wearing his raincoat while he ate, which he did rapidly, buttering his roll deftly and using it to load his fork with Salisbury steak and mashed potato. He was hurrying, he told his grandfather, because he did not want to hold up the train.

"Leave it until you're a little older," said Mr. Thorston. I like to imagine that when Mr. Thorston said this Mason stopped eating and stared at him with an expression on his face of pained disbelief.

Eventually Mason derailed a train that happened to be moving a shipment of top-secret matériel for the U.S. Army from Texas to San Diego. He did this in partnership with a girl from his school who was not the child of a movie star. They then went underground. Federal marshals hunted for them all over the country. Mason was spotted in Chicago but then he disappeared. A young man they suspected of being Mason looked very much like him in profile. He had flattop black hair and Mason's disdainful, flared nostrils. Seen from the front, however, the suspect was too fat to be Mason. He looked like Mason trying to make a face by inflating his cheeks and turning his bottom lip inside out.

In newspaper headlines right after it happened Mason was identified as a grandson of the Golden West. Mason's mother's love life was depicted as part of the larger picture. It was like the love life of a movie star. Nightclub photographs were published showing her in the company of other women's husbands. She always wore the same expression of helpless surprise.

The fugitives hid out on farms and in cheap boardinghouses. They fueled their flight with amphetamines. It was Mr. Thorston's guess that Mason was growing old very fast. The couple held up a diner in Huntsville, Texas. They were doomed. They were captured at last in Topeka, Kansas, not far from the Menninger Clinic, where Mason was committed soon after for a prolonged series of electric shock treatments.

They brought him home in an ambulance. He was now the victim of a degenerative kidney ailment caused by an excessive use of drugs. Mr. Thorston installed him across the hall from the room in which Mrs. Thorston lay dying of cancer. Here he remained. The doctors estimated that he would live for from five to seven more years. Mrs. Thorston gradually lost her strength entirely and died. Mr. Thorston, soon to be eighty-five, continued to enjoy uninterrupted good health.

When the weather was clement Mason sat out on the lawn and received visitors during the afternoon. He wore a richly brocaded green silk dressing gown over his pajamas. He was now white-skinned and fat. He wore his hair in a brush cut. Each week a girl from a local beauty parlor came to shape his hair and manicure his nails. His manner, though scornful, was never anything but dignified. Most days he stayed upstairs in his room. In the evenings, when he felt up to it, he came downstairs to dine with Mr. Thorston.

They were served by the South American cook. They ate well and accompanied their meals with a bottle of claret from Mr. Thorston's vineyards. After dinner they watched television. Sometimes Mr. Thorston took Mason out for dinner to a Spanish restaurant in the neighborhood where flamenco was performed for the customers during dinner. On these outings Mason wore a red smoking jacket belted over a pair of slacks, and bedroom slippers. Mr. Thorston always reserved a ringside table, and the manager invariably instructed the dancers to perform, for Mason, the Habanera from the opera *Carmen*.

Mr. Thorston understood that Mason wanted to see the Grand Tetons before he died. Together they planned the trip. Mr. Thorston found a train that made a round-trip excursion seemingly designed expressly to enable invalids to view the Grand Tetons. The proposed route took the train north along the Columbia River up into Canada, through the Canadian Rockies, and down into Montana. It passed through Yellowstone Park and then along a spur that took in great vistas of the Grand Tetons, rejoined the main line at Jackson, Wyoming, and headed back to the Pacific coast. Mr. Thorston arranged with the railroad to have Mason's meals served to him in his compartment. He arranged for Mason to occupy a double compartment equipped with a shower and an armchair in case he felt like sitting up. He also bought the boy a bagful of Zane Grey westerns to read on the trip. Together they went to the station. Mr. Thorston stayed with Mason until the whistle blew, and then watched as the train slid away. Mason, propped up on white-sleeved pullman pillows, leaned forward to wave down from his berth to the old man on the platform.

The trip was a success. Mason sent Mr. Thorston a postcard from Jackson, Wyoming. "Tetons have Big Tops," he wrote. He came home on a catafalque.

The Butler

Remember the Outhwaites? They lived in Coconut Grove. They were well off but not as rich as they wanted to be. Every night Mrs. Outhwaite stuck a pin in the body of a voodoo doll that represented the image of Mr. Outhwaite's rich elderly cousin, known as Aunt Alice, who was believed by the Outhwaites to have named Mr. Outhwaite as a beneficiary in her will. This turned out to be the case. Aunt Alice died and much to the annoyance of other surviving relations bequeathed her entire estate to Mr. Outhwaite.

The Outhwaites without further delay purchased a Moroccan-style palace down the coast that had been in disrepair for decades and hired a set designer to re-create its original glamour. Mr. Outhwaite had met this man across the bridge table during a cruise of the Caribbean on which he had once escorted Aunt Alice. The set designer transformed the ruined palace into a sumptuous showplace. He restored the tiled fountains in the courtyards and supervised the decoration of rooms. Each bedchamber in the palace was designed as for a visiting sultan. The job of restoration was continuous and the set designer became a permanent guest of the Outhwaites. He was to be found at most of their lunch parties.

Jacques, the Haitian butler, was another fixture of the Outhwaite lunch parties. He was a discovery of the set designer. He could be seen moving nimbly about in the courtyard arcade correcting the seasoning of the luncheon casseroles. Jacques wore a white jacket. His tasks were varied. He adjusted the spray of the courtyard fountains. He modulated the Vivaldi that was piped via a speaker system throughout the palace. He kept the palace supplied with fresh fish. Jacques traveled with the Outhwaites. In Paris Jacques, who was installed in a *pension,* appeared before the Outhwaites each morning in his white jacket. Over the remains of breakfast in the living room of their hotel suite the Outhwaites issued him a set of instructions for the day. He was called upon to do things like order opera tickets and walk the dogs. He also accompanied the Outhwaites on shopping expeditions so that he might supervise the delivery of their packages safely back to the hotel. The Outhwaites often complimented the set designer on having discovered Jacques. The set designer agreed that Jacques was an unusual find.

You don't find butlers like Jacques just anywhere, he told the Outh-waites.

The set designer was a busy man much in demand, it seemed, in the entertainment world. He brought a taste of excitement to life at the palace. Mr. Outhwaite, especially, liked to have him on hand. He gave Mr. Outhwaite tips about Broadway theatrical productions. Mr. Outh-waite had expressed an interest in backing Broadway shows with some of the money he had inherited from Aunt Alice, and this was something about which the set designer, who had suggested the idea to begin with, was in a good position to advise him.

Jacques made Mrs. Outhwaite his special responsibility. Mrs. Outh-waite had a philosophical turn of mind. She was an original thinker. Jacques made a note of this. He and Mrs. Outhwaite took long walks to-gether on the beach so that Mrs. Outhwaite could collect shells while they discussed world federalism. Jacques more than once was seen emerging from the public library in the company of Mrs. Outhwaite. He programmed courses for her in history and political science and togeth-er they studied the atlas. Jacques stimulated in Mrs. Outhwaite a de-sire to visit less-well-known parts of the world.

Jacques, as it happened, also played bridge. This came as a welcome surprise to the Outhwaites. They were avid bridge players. They paired off Jacques with the set designer in palace bridge games. The Outh-waites played for ten cents a point. They were prepared to advance Jacques a week's salary when he joined them for bridge. Mrs. Outh-waite in particular, although she disapproved of wealth on principle and felt that it was distributed unevenly throughout the world, was merciless about the acquisition of other people's money, especially when it happened to be Jacques's unearned salary. In the course of time rath-er large sums of money came to be involved and they settled accounts on a monthly basis. Mrs. Outhwaite was occasionally shocked to find herself paying out two or three times the amount of Jacques's regular salary. On the whole the opponents seemed well matched, however, and the foursome settled down to an intensely serious bridge game with an ongoing score and no end in sight.

The Outhwaites devoted themselves to bridge now when they traveled. They were drawn away from European civilization and its distractions to the Middle East and Africa. They sent Jacques ahead of them with the dogs and the car and flew in later with the set designer after Jacques had secured suitable accommodations. Sometimes Jacques found a local driver to take them on extensive side trips by car. He sat up front next to the driver and prepared snacks for the traveling party. He poured daiquiris from a Thermos into plastic cups, which he handed over into the back seat to Mr. Outhwaite and then to the set designer, although not to Mrs. Outhwaite, because she never drank anything alcoholic. At night they sat down immediately after dinner to resume the bridge game wherever they found themselves.

The Outhwaites began to lose badly to the Haitian and the set designer in Cairo, where they lived grandly in a villa on the Nile. They covered their early losses with holdings in Canadian timber. They lost all their General Motors stock playing duplicate bridge the following winter in Marrakesh. They played for twenty-five cents a point in the Canary Islands and broke even. In the Cote d'Ivoire, however, once again they lost badly. They always returned to the palace. One year the Outhwaites shipped their green Chrysler station wagon over to Kinshasa and drove into the jungle with Jacques and the set designer. Months later, they emerged. Quietly they returned home. They sold the cars and most of the furniture. They auctioned off their rugs and most of their silver. They dumped the palace onto a depressed market and took a considerable loss on their investment. The bridge game was over. The set designer retired to Capri. The Haitian stayed on long enough to help the Outhwaites move into a rented house with their dogs. He was ever the butler.

Heir

Maximillian, heir to an American cement-manufacturing fortune, visited Italy throughout his boyhood and once spent a summer at a Fascist youth camp in the Italian Lake District. This experience made a great impression on him. Afterward he made a papier-mâché sculpture of Mussolini, which was used as an illustration in an American magazine for teenagers. Later, at the outbreak of World War II, the illustration was somehow discovered and used against him. By then Maximillian was a college graduate and a member of ROTC. When he joined the army he was put on a train for new Orleans where, he was told, he would receive his commission. Somewhere in Louisiana, however, the train stopped and Maximillian was ordered to get off it. He was taken under guard to an isolated internment camp surrounded by barbed wire where U.S. citizens who held suspicious views were confined during the war. Maximillian was imprisoned in this camp with Marxists, Nazi sympathizers, and other political suspects for nearly a year. His mother, who traveled in exalted social circles, finally prevailed upon a general of her acquaintance to arrange for his release, and Maximillian was placed in Army Intelligence. After the defeat of Mussolini he was sent to Italy to interrogate Italian prisoners of war, an assignment for which he was highly qualified because he spoke fluent Italian. Maximillian received an honorable discharge from the army. He never referred to his experience in the internment camp.

Maximillian married an Austrian countess after the war at a high mass in Saint Peter's Cathedral in Rome, where he happened to be studying to become a sculptor. He was not a Catholic, but the romantic, theatrical quality of the Roman Catholic ceremony in the Vatican appealed to Maximillian immensely. The marriage lasted six or seven years. When it broke up Maximillian was back in the United States working in the family cement business. The divorce was a long, drawn-out affair and involved a large financial settlement. Maximillian finally ended the marriage by going to a guest ranch near Reno, Nevada, where he established the six-week residence required of people from out of state who go there to obtain a quick divorce. There he had an opportunity to observe cowboys on horseback riding the range. Subsequently he married a woman from Argentina and devoted himself to making clay models in preparation for a larger-than-life monument he planned to sculpt of a lone cowhand on horseback.

Maximillian also made medallions. He alternated between making medallions and constructing his great monument to the American West. He made silver and bronze medallions. He liked to discolor them with verdigris so that they took on a properly aged appearance. His medallions were copies of Roman coins embossed with the profiles of emperors. His favorite emperors were Caesar Augustus and Quintus Fabius Maximus. He intensely disliked modern sculpture and design. He disliked also the modesty of small medallions, which he referred to contemptuously as buttonhole art. His own medallions were the size of paperweights. He celebrated the heroic aspirations of man. Maximillian's taste was decidedly nineteenth-century Victorian imperialist, although the roots of his cowboy monument would be found in *fin-de-siècle* American romanticism.

Maximillian's medallions stood little chance of being exhibited in serious collections, although he sold some of them as curiosities at several European expositions. A vanity press eventually published a *catalogue raisonné* of his work as a medallionist with an introduction in praise of Maximillian's sculpture by a reputable representational American artist. This was possibly the best that Maximillian could expect for his work. He nevertheless continued to submit his medallions to museums and galleries, which sooner or later always rejected them. Maximillian's monumental sculpture promised to fare better. It was a far more impressive effort than his medallions, heroic in scope. A giant sculpture of a cowboy on horseback was a notion with some institutional appeal and one that, although still in the planning stage, drew admiring comparisons to the work of Giovanni Bernini and Ivan Meštrović. A great monument, however, takes a long time to sculpt and even then is a difficult project to launch without a commission. Maximillian wanted a more immediate audience for his endeavors.

He and his wife hit on the idea of casting a medallion to the memory of Eva Perón. Maximillian's brother-in-law was a part-time officer of the Argentine diplomatic corps. He was assigned on occasion to diplomatic missions in the United States, where he maintained a permanent residence. On behalf of Maximillian he organized, through his foreign ministry, an official delegation to Buenos Aires so that Maximillian could present his medallion in person to Juan Perón. The party consist-ed of Maximillian, his brother-in-law, and two other delegates from the Argentine. When they arrived in Buenos Aires their number was swelled by personal representatives of the caudillo.

The delegation flew down there in great style. Maximillian presented his medallion to Perón at the entrance to the city at a wreath-laying ceremony commemorating the birthday of the dictator's late wife. The event may have been scheduled expressly for the purpose of Maximil-lian's presentation. A full-dress honor guard of Argentine army and navy officers attended the ceremony, along with officials of the Argen-tine government and the diplomatic representatives of several Latin American countries. The embassy of the United States did not send a representative on the principle that it never participates in private rit-uals arranged and financed wholly or in part by American citizens through foreign diplomatic channels. This attitude infuriated Maximil-lian, who was also offended because the event was not reported in the U.S. press. It seemed to him hypocritical of the United States, which had supported Perón publicly for many years, now to repudiate an American who had the audacity to honor the woman who had done so much to keep him in power. Maximillian's medallion was exhibited for a time under glass at the presidential palace in Buenos Aires and later was entombed with other relics and personal effects of Eva Perón in a special vault set aside for that purpose in the national cemetery.

Maximillian continued to work on his sculpture of the cowboy on horseback when he returned from his South American junket. He hired a Hollywood press agent to sell it to any one of several civic and educa-tional institutions in Texas and California, but the press agent was no art dealer. The finished monument was never sold or even exhibited. Maximillian and his wife by this time had become interested in Indian spiritualism. They joined the ashram of a guru who traveled all over the United States to visit his followers and who, when absent on his travels, would telephone long distance and deliver homilies to his ash-ram over a public address system. Maximillian met and became romantically attached to a divorcée who also attended the ashram. Maximillian's wife, when her attention was drawn to this fact, hired private detectives to follow the couple. Soon Maximillian was again involved in a divorce suit. He did not marry the divorcée, however, though the guru did not gaze unkindly upon their liaison. Nor did Maximillian lose much of his fortune in the divorce settlement with his Argentine wife. Quite wisely, on the advice of his accountant, Maximillian had rented furnished houses throughout this second marriage, and the better part of his inheritance, still to come, was locked in a trust fund controlled by his mother, who lived grandly in the South of France on the interest of the invested capital.

The Nephew

Count Rudolph Von Redwig lived with a rich older woman who, he said, was his aunt. He never hesitated to tell people that his aunt supported him. He boasted about his aunt's wealth. He volunteered the information that she had once been a girl friend of Al Capone. He also asserted that his aunt was a cousin of Greta Garbo. He said that she had invented and patented an internationally known cough syrup during the 1930s. She was a chemist, he said. She'd hit upon a compound made up of various antianalgesics and the root of a little-known South American plant. The cough syrup quadrupled the fortune she had inherited from her father, according to Rudy. He repelled people with his eager candor. He let it be known that every morning his aunt put a crisp new one-hundred-dollar bill under his plate before he came down for breakfast. He informed everyone in his good-natured way that his aunt had ordered him a custom-built Rolls-Royce convertible for Christmas and on Christmas Day he drove it to the polo grounds to show it off. Rudy made no effort to suppress the keen delight he felt about owning it. He was unconcerned that others might not be able to share his enthusiasm.

Rudy's aunt was an aging Valkyrie. She clothed her immense frame in loose gowns that billowed about her to the floor. Her thick white tresses cascaded to her shoulders from the top of her head like a cotton wig. She had the brutally swollen, purplish face and cornered watchfulness of a veteran prizefighter. She was someone who liked to have a good time, you could see that. She bared her teeth when she laughed. She was not choosy about the people Rudy brought back to their apartment for drinks. She might well have been Al Capone's moll. It was hard to believe that she had invented a cough remedy, though. Rudy she had hired away from his job as a security guard at a Las Vegas bank, it was said, while she was visiting Nevada to obtain a divorce from husband number eight. In Mexico you hear all kinds of things about people. Now, it was said, Rudy supplied the old girl with a lively social schedule and kept her company throughout the evening until she drank him under the table.

Rudy and his aunt lived in an apartment hotel on the outskirts of Guadalajara. Every morning after breakfast Rudy visited an exclusive

81

men's hairstyling salon run by an ex-Nazi barber, where he exchanged his one-hundred-dollar bill for black-market pesos. While there he treated himself to a shave and shampoo and a manicure. He arrived at the polo grounds around noon in a cloud of expensive after-shave lotion. He wore an unbelted vicuña polo coat over his riding clothes. He always carried a grip containing a fresh change of clothes. He left a small pile of gold furnishings on the top shelf of his locker. This consisted of a gold wristwatch that he claimed had been given to him by the king of Saudi Arabia who, he said, was a close friend of his aunt; a gold medallion on a gold chain, which he said had been personally blessed by the pope, also a friend of his aunt; and a weighty gold signet ring bearing a stamp of his initials, which one scornful polo player said stood for Rolls Von Royce.

He was a five-goal player. He played with intense skill. He was an incredibly gifted horseman. He packed immense power. He was possessed of lightning reflexes. He covered the field with great speed. He was an especially good player in high altitudes. He was indispensable in team matches against Mexico City. He was better than most of the other players on the team. He claimed to have been the captain of a polo team in northern India during the war. He had learned how to ride as a child in Arizona, he said, had played polo as a teenager in boarding school, and then later, when in college, he had played varsity polo even though, as he all too candidly confessed, he had failed most of his courses and had only been allowed to stay on and graduate because his aunt had donated the chemistry lab. He spoke convincingly about the great polo players of the 1930s, men like Wild Bill Ylvisaker, the maharaja of Jaipur, and Tommy Hitchcock. He said that he had played polo with them all. He asserted that he had once saved the life of the maharaja of Screech Galore, in India, during the war.

Each year Rudy and his aunt disappeared for three or four months during the Mexican rainy season. When the count returned he often could not recall exactly where they had been. He explained that he seldom paid any attention to his whereabouts because so many of the countries they visited looked alike. Sometimes they went to Riyadh to see the king of Saudi Arabia. Once they went to Bangkok to visit the king and queen of Thailand. One year they reappeared after a long absence and Rudy told everyone that he and his aunt had been on a swing through Africa, where they had traveled up the Nile on a chartered river steamer. When closely questioned about the Nile the count was rather evasive. He volunteered, however, to project a movie that had been shot during the expedition. A number of curious polo players attended the screening, which was held after dinner in the clubhouse on a white sheet that had been provided for the purpose and suspended from a rafter on the ceiling. Rudy accompanied the movie with an informal narration of his own. As it unreeled, the film documented group portraits of naked, potbellied tribesmen lined up on the riverbank and giraffes loping across a southern plain. A wildebeest floating in the river, which Rudy said his aunt had shot from the deck of the steamer, could be seen sliding away downstream. It is being devoured by the swift Nile current, Rudy said. Shots of Rudy and his aunt were indistinct, although Rudy was able to indicate one or another of them on the screen, in the distance. There's my aunt, he said at one point. A dugout canoe could be seen in the vast sweep of the river. Two people, barely discernible, were hunched at either end of the shallow vessel. Something created a turbulence in the water. There occurred a violent splashing. His aunt, Rudy said, was beating a crocodile to death with her oar. The movie ended with an unexplained aerial shot of Victoria Falls, then slipped off the reel, but not before disclosing, with a sort of wink, the colophon of Castle Films, Ltd., dated 1935, which explained the speckled, sepia quality of the photography.

One winter day the polo team crowded into automobiles and drove up to Mexico City for a team match. Rudy, of course, was urged to come along and so he did with his customary good cheer. He was not aware that Screech Galore would be playing as a guest of honor for the Mexican team, although this was generally known and had been kept a secret from the count by his teammates. When they arrived at Campo Marte the maharaja released a little scream. He embraced the count before the disembarking Guadalajara team. Screech, as he was known, seemed to have gone mad. He pounded the red-faced count on his back, then he gripped Rudy by the hand and pumped it furiously up and down. He turned to the onlookers. "This man saved my life," announced the guest of honor. Twenty years ago, he declared, in India, during the war.

Rudy and his aunt were fixtures on the social scene in Guadalajara for a number of years. You could see them barreling along in the Rolls-Royce together on their way to a cocktail party or a wine tasting. Rudy's aunt wore dark glasses. She sat beside him in the front seat. She liked to rest one bare, white elbow on the window sill. Rudy handled the big car like a professional chauffeur. He always wore black driving gloves. They lived in Guadalajara, he told people, because his aunt liked the dry climate. He confessed that he preferred the moist breezes of Acapulco. One year the count returned from a particularly long absence without his aunt and made immediate preparations to move their household belongings to Acapulco. That climate was more to his taste, he explained to the polo team, and now that his aunt was no longer living, as he put it, he saw no reason to delay the move. He had purchased a villa in a newly developed community called Las Brisas, where the rooms were built on a descending sequence of landscaped terraces open to sun, sea, and rain, unprotected by windows or doors against the tropical seasons. He was, as always, disturbing in his candor. His aunt, he said, had fallen overboard and been devoured by piranha in a matter of minutes during an excursion they had undertaken up the Amazon River. Subsequently a short *New York Times* obituary appeared in a Mexico City English-language daily newspaper confirming the death of Rudy's aunt. HEDVIG VON REDWIG IS DEAD was the article headline. Rudy's aunt indeed had been a girl friend at one time of Al Capone, according to this account. She had invented a famous cough remedy, also. She was, evidently, a papal countess. Her title had been bestowed upon her by her good friend the pope. She was a close personal friend of ruling monarchs as well, the article reported, including the kings of Thailand and Saudi Arabia. She was survived, the brief report concluded, by her nephew, Count Rudolph Von Redwig. There was no mention of Greta Garbo.

Byron N.Y.
7788

Baby Boy

I first trained my sights on Baby Boy Jarratt as he came down the gangway of the *Trondheim* late one night in Venice. That was the fabulous summer of '62 when it seemed that everyone had discovered the pastime of Mediterranean yachting all over again. The *Trondheim*, Har Osvaldsen's minesweeper, was riding at anchor off the Grand Canal. We used to sit on the top deck of the *Caveat Emptor* and watch the comings and goings aboard the *Trondheim*, hoping for a glimpse of the fabulous Baby Boy Jarratt or at least a chance to steal a look at one of the Nazi war criminals Har Osvaldsen was said to be hiding on board his ship. The side of the *Trondheim* was brightly lit at night and we could recognize Baby Boy at once. He was wearing a white dinner jacket over his shoulders like a cape, a difficult thing to do at night while trotting down a stairway to board a vaporetto, although I don't imagine for a minute that Baby Boy was probably even aware of the impression of supreme nonchalance he created. He was in such a hurry. He carried a drink in one hand. He nimbly leaped aboard the pitching launch, which promptly lumbered off across the dark water toward the stagelit Piazza San Marco.

He did, after all, look like a baby boy. He had a rosy complexion that when sunburned made him appear fevered. He had a fierce malicious smile and bright, wide-awake blue eyes. He was by then such a prodigy that one tended to forget that he was the son of a socially quite prominent, rich American mother, Mrs. Auchincloss Bosshard, who lived in Oyster Bay, and her first husband, E. Clarendon Jarratt, the English bridge architect. Baby Boy attended Eton. He spoke French. As a child he spent his summers on the French side of the English Channel. His father, in fact, had first introduced Baby Boy to the world of professional gambling one summer in Monte Carlo, where he had gone to supervise the reconstruction of a railroad bridge. There Baby Boy had learned how to play chemin de fer. The number ten turned out to be Baby Boy's lucky number. He became a baccarat whiz, and the rest is history. He was the toast of Mayfair at the age of fifteen. He broke the bank so many times that all the private gaming clubs in London closed their doors to him on the pitiful grounds that he was underage. Why, then, had they allowed him to play to his heart's content in the first place? Thereafter, Baby Boy played exclusively on private yachts.

The *Trondheim* slipped out of Venice late at night on the thirty-first of July with Baby Boy on board. We heard later that he had planned to leave the *Trondheim* the next day to join a new game later that week on a yacht moored off Sestri Levante, but he never made it. He awoke on the afternoon of the first of August in the Adriatic port of Pula. He had an awful hangover. He demanded, but did not receive, a suitable explanation. Nobody on board seemed to know what was going on. Osvaldsen had gone ashore to visit the war museum. Somebody took the time to explain to Baby Boy, in a low voice—everyone spoke in a low voice aboard the *Trondheim*—that with Osvaldsen you never knew where you might surface next. This was totally unacceptable to Baby Boy. He marched off and found a telegraph office somewhere in the dusty little port town. There he wrote out a message on a telegram form and addressed it to his father's solicitor in London. BABY BOY KID-NAPPED ON TRONDHEIM he printed in thick black capital letters. He signed it MASTERSON, which was the name used by the captain of the *Trondheim*. The woman who took the message refused to accept payment in Italian lire. Baby Boy was desperate. "Then give me back the bloody form," he shouted. She obdurately refused to understand him. There wasn't much time left. He unstrapped his watch and shoved it under the bars of the telegraph window with his fingers. "Then take this," he shouted. The woman looked doubtful. Baby Boy fled back to the harbor through a maze of unfamiliar streets. The last thing he needed was to find himself penniless in some godforsaken Dalmatian backwater. He achieved the *Trondheim* just in time for cocktails on the afterdeck. The atmosphere was sumptuous and muted. He decided not to betray his anxiety by asking any more hostile questions. The *Trondheim* manservant took his order and returned shortly with a ruby-red Negroni cocktail on a silver tray. The mountains had taken on a dusky, purplish hue. The air, as the *Trondheim* glided slowly out into the Adriatic, was clear and invigorating. The Negronis kept coming. Suddenly Jarratt was exhilarated. He forgot altogether his earlier outrage. By the time he was sipping at his third Negroni it seemed to him that the telegram incident had taken place in a distant primeval bosk and had involved a miniature version of his present self.

Baby Boy fell in love with a sulky French protégée of Har Osvaldsen by the name of Anik. It happened unexpectedly on the night of Pula. In the days that followed they swam in the late morning and lay in the sun on the foredeck, and in the afternoon, below decks, in Anik's cabin, they took long, drugged naps. Lunch abroad the *Trondheim* was a smorgasbord. Dinner was a four-course formal sit-down meal taken in the dining salon at a mahogany table at which Captain Masterson presided in the absence of Har Osvaldsen, who remained sequestered in his compartment, where he conducted business, it was believed, by shortwave radio. Masterson looked like a sheriff. He wore a khaki uniform. He was a robust man of the sea who claimed to be a Scot, although we were later informed by the captain of the *Caveat Emptor* that he was really a gunrunner from Cicero, Illinois. He had hairy black eyebrows and swiftly darting brown eyes and a swarthy complexion, none of which would be Scottish, taken altogether, would they, now, the captain of the *Caveat* wanted to know. Masterson wore a revolver in a black leather holster at the hip of his whipcord trousers. He ate with gusto, wiped his mouth often with his white damask napkin, and drank wine voluminously. The *Trondheim* manservant waited to fill Masterson's glass with Burgundy from a cut-glass decanter as soon as the captain emptied it. Jolly Captain Mac. He tyrannized the *Trondheim* guests with tales of his exploits at sea as a freighter captain in the Indian Ocean. None of the guests dared to interrupt him, and as a result it was hard for them to say anything to one another while they ate. They were cursed, the *Trondheim* passengers, with being spoken about all the time by the whole world in salacious and obscenely speculative language, while locked in silence together aboard the *Trondheim*. Aspers Wenzel, the gregarious Danish killer; the melancholy but flirtatious Mrs. Watling-Mellors, who had known better days in Kenya; the infamous Duchess of A., exotic in black, whose liaisons with London bobbies were just then being serialized in the British press; Manfred Heydrich, who, contrary to what we all thought then, had actually been a most resourceful foe of the Third Reich; Baby Boy; Anik; Jean Claude Grenier, the scandal-plagued French tennis ace—they all felt constrained from speaking, except to ask for the salt. They went about the ship on tiptoe. They had furtive affairs. At night they concentrated strictly on cards.

Masterson alone possessed keys to all the doors aboard the *Trond-heim*. After dinner he unlocked a door in the paneled wall of the dining salon that opened into the gambling parlor. Though not a baccarat player himself he nevertheless set the scene, adjusted the lighting, checked the seating arrangements, and conferred with the croupiers. He moved briskly about like a big cat. His cheeks were flushed from all the wine he had drunk. He hardly ever appeared to have consumed too much, although once Baby Boy happened to see his eyes cloud over. On this occasion the captain's words slurred into mush, very briefly, and Baby Boy was quite sure the man had begun to transmogrify into an ape. His hands, at that moment, had appeared to swell and darken.

Anik either could not or would not explain to Baby Boy Jarratt exactly why she was on board, although he repeatedly tried to get her to tell him. She tormented him with her moods. They were rarely apart. At night, in the gaming room, Anik hung onto his shoulder with both hands while he played. Purely as an act of gallantry Baby Boy turned over his winnings to Anik for safekeeping, and at dawn they drank Greek brandy together on the afterdeck and watched the sunrise. But at lunch beside the topdeck pool Anik often spurned him to sit with Jean Claude Grenier, a cumbersome blond pederast. They spoke French and became cross when Baby Boy sauntered over to join them with his plate of hot shrimp curry and his glass of white wine. Conversation dwindled and died. Social intercourse was blocked at every turn aboard the *Trondheim*.

Indeed this was one yacht trip that Baby Boy sometimes wished he had never taken. He went from one emotional extreme to another all day long. He was always trying to open doors that were locked. Half the time he felt like a prisoner on a submarine. He was both locked out and locked in. His love affair with Anik had thickened. She thrashed around her stateroom, which was open to sea and sky, stirring up an exciting storm of tissue paper. *Je suis emprisonnée* she would turn and, seized with fury, hurl at Baby Boy Jarratt, who was standing spellbound before her in all his birthday glory. She hated the Frenchman. She hated the endless nothingness. She hated the bloodsucking captain. She hated watching him sucking the life out of Har Osvaldsen, his prisoner on this cruise without end. He throws him chunks of meat, she told Baby Boy. They stood before each other in the stateroom. She was calm and lucid. He throws my body in there. Some one of these days soon enough he will throw you in there, too, she told him. *Comme le tenniste.* "But that's insane," cried Baby Boy Jarratt. "We have to get out of here." She laughed. She had all his winnings.

In Dubrovnik Baby Boy awoke to an empty ship. The *Trondheim* appeared to have been abandoned. The other passengers were nowhere about. Baby Boy, hung over yet again, was troubled by foreboding. He took a trolley into town and hurried in his sandals through the hot somnolent city. He sighted the tennis player: burnished hair, white shorts, white Italian loafers. He was taking snapshots, squatting to do so, of two local lads who were posing arm in arm on the steps of a cathedral. This vision of the French Adonis somehow reassured Baby Boy. He hurried on to find his heart's truelove. She was out at the Hotel Excelsior on the swimming terrace, lying next to Gigi Grimaldi, a short, sunburned, balding Brazilian boyfriend of hers with a potbelly, who had been pursuing her in his own yacht, *Flying Cobra,* ever since their well-publicized fight in a bar on the *Croisette* in Cannes the previous April.

As it happened I was there when Baby Boy appeared at the top of the steps. It was my second look at Baby Boy that summer. He was tall and looked slightly chinless in his wraparound dark glasses, which bulged on his face. Truly it was as though a god had decided to make a brief appearance. The sky overhead darkened dramatically. The Adriatic spanked the sea wall and sloshed onto the terrace, where it seethed among the bathers. Baby Boy surveyed the scene. He sighted Anik. She was combing the hair on Gigi's chest with her fingers over in the corner. She stood up when he came over. They held a furious dialogue. The air burned. "I don't want your lies. I want my money," Baby Boy announced in a minatory voice. He turned heel and strode across the terrace whence he'd come. Anik hugged her arms. *Allez alors allez, Bébé,* she jeered at his swiftly retreating figure.

On board the *Trondheim* he stood before her locked stateroom door behind which, he was certain, he would find somewhere concealed among cans of hairspray his considerable winnings. He was contemplating kicking in the door with the heel of his sandal when Har Osvaldsen glided right along the wall of the passageway in a silk kimono and grasped Baby Boy by the wrist. His grip felt like cold steel. The current of his passion pulsed unpleasantly into Baby Boy Jarratt. He smelled of bath powder. Don't leave me, he said. Stay here. Stay with me always. I have everything. Play! Play chemin de fer! Win! Oh win my Baby Boy my darling win! He grinned, and Baby Boy saw diamonds where Osvaldsen's teeth should have been. "Get," said Baby Boy. He ripped away his arm. He then began what seemed like an interminable search for escape. Some hallways came to a dead end. Others seemed endless or took him up short flights to locked stateroom doors. Engines rumbled underneath him. He caught his breath. There had to be some way to get out of here. He seemed repeatedly, later, in his waking memory, to have been flying down a wildly pitching corridor, which was like a vortex, toward a waiter carrying a tray who then exploded with fright, dropped his tray, and screamed as though he'd seen a rat. He finally found a companionway. He hardly knew whether to laugh or cry while, exhausted, he relaxed against the teak-paneled wall and mopped his brow with the back of his hand. He then threw himself upon the stairs and scrambled furiously up them.

Har Osvaldsen was seated on the afterdeck receiving a delegation of three plainclothes detectives who had driven down the entire length of Yugoslavia in pursuit of the *Trondheim* and who had come on board to investigate the kidnap charge telegraphed from Pula by Captain Masterson. Masterson was standing beside the throne at Har Osvaldsen's right elbow coughing into his fist like an embarrassed Scotsman, if there is such a thing, or was he laughing uncontrollably? Baby Boy couldn't tell. Har Osvaldsen was explaining patiently in simple declarative English sentences that he had no interest whatever in baby boys. Baby Boy took a chill intake of breath when he heard that! He stood, frozen, at the doorway from the lounge onto the deck and watched. Har Osvaldsen's slippered feet rested on a footstool. Thin Turkish rugs were scattered about on the polished deck. One of the Croats, a brutish man in a dark green business suit, who wore dark glasses and a shiny flesh-toned plastic neck brace, went down before Osvaldsen in mock veneration and with theatrical flourish placed Baby Boy Jarratt's wristwatch across the magnate's knee. Masterson shot him. Next thing Baby Boy knew, Masterson was crouched behind the throne and Osvaldsen was crawling toward him across the shiny wooden deck. The two surviving plainclothesmen were beating a retreat and turning to fire at them with handguns as they went. "Next thing you know," muttered Osvaldsen, who was getting to his feet beside Baby Boy Jarratt, but that was all he said because he had been mortally wounded and now slumped on the deck. Masterson bounded like an ape up the stairs that led to the bridge. The detectives had gone for reinforcements. The *Trondheim* pulled away from the dock under the sure hand of Captain Masterson. The detectives roared back along the freight-loading dock in an army truck in time to see the *Trondheim* exhaust holes emit rich billows of black diesel smoke as she began to pick up speed. Soldiers from the army truck jumped down and began to fire at them with automatic weapons. The *Trondheim* was soon gathering speed on the open sea. The port city huddled under a black sky. Flashes of machine-gun fire sparked on the shore.

Baby Boy stood on the foredeck in the oncoming night. He had faced the awful truth. Life was incredibly exciting on the *Trondheim*. He could stay on it with Captain Masterson for the rest of his life if he wanted, crashing from one ocean to another, running a superb gambling operation. He loved being locked up. He adored Anik. He adored Yugoslavia. He adored the *Trondheim*. He adored his life. He could never be happy. Drink had become an almost besetting vice. Drink, as much as lust, had obviously brought Har Osvaldsen, that leprotic wretch, to his sad conclusion. Two dead bodies on the afterdeck. Such were the thoughts of the Honorable Henry William Edward Clarence Jarratt during the long storm-tossed night that followed. The day after was serene and icy calm as they cruised slowly along the Albanian coast in the shadow of a distant mountain wall. In Corfu the summer was in full swing. Some of Baby Boy's Eton friends were playing cricket on the green. He went away with them. Subsequently he became a successful London banker. Quite some time afterward I happened to see the *Trondheim* again entirely by chance in the harbor of Dar es Salaam, but that's another story.

Charades

Irene was a daughter of the frontier. Her mother, who was part Cherokee, took in sewing for the wives of landowners in the Salinas Valley. Irene was the offspring of her love affair with a passionate roustabout of Irish descent who eventually got lucky and married the widow of a local millionaire. He now lived in style with this woman in Pebble Beach, where he was famous for his bonhomie. He spent his days going to lunch parties; by night he played the role of drunken companion to his rich elderly wife, who happened to be crippled. He hardly had time left over for Irene and her hard-bitten mother, but he never forgot them. They were the dark, hidden side of his life. He regularly sent Irene's mother his rich wife's discarded cocktail dresses, which she altered and then wore at her sewing table while she mended the somewhat less fashionable clothes of her clientele. She looked like a smart, tough divorcée in those black French hand-me-downs. It was a role she was content to play even though she and Irene's father had never exchanged vows.

Irene received no formal education. At an age when most children are learning how to write a complete sentence, Irene went to work for her mother, who took it upon herself to educate Irene while they toiled away together over the sewing. Her mother never bothered to teach Irene how to read or write. Instead she taught her the fashion business. She made Irene commit to memory the styles of French fashion designers that appeared on the pages of *Vogue* and *Harper's Bazaar.* She used to drill Irene on the terms used by couturiers when they referred to particular patterns and cuts of cloth. She graded her daughter on her ability to match colors and textures. She ripped apart her clients' dresses at the seams and made Irene stitch them up again by hand. She taught Irene how to quickly size up a dress and the woman who wore it and the man who had paid for it. This brought her in due course to the subject of men. She told Irene everything she knew about rich men. She placed great stress on the word *rich.* Rich men, she told Irene, are capable of resisting all but the best French perfume. Rich men look for flaws but they want to be fooled. And so forth. This inevitably brought her back once again to the matter of clothes. She placed a far higher value on clothes than on jewelry, for instance. You may knock a rich man out for a few seconds with a well-cut diamond, but you can knock him dead with a hemline, she told Irene. By the time she was eighteen, Irene was all set to make her way in the world.

The old roustabout showed up one fine April afternoon. He had driven down to tell Irene's mother that his wife was dying and to announce that he was ready, at last, to offer his hand to her in marriage. This was her cue. At last! she retorted. At last! You think I want to be your wife now? Not so fast, paleface. Give me time. She squinted, inhaled deeply on her cigarette, tapped it against the ashtray with her index finger. Then she looked at him pleasantly. I don't want you to marry me yet, she said. First, I want you to take Irene. Take her into your house. Do with her as you will. She is yours as much as she is mine. Only make her yours. Take her to your heart. Do as I say. No one has to know. Then when the time is right I will come to you if you both need me. The old man was aghast. Irene stepped forth from the shadows. He beheld her for the first time. Her beauty astonished him. She had a wide Mongolian face, green eyes, and a radiant Irish complexion. He felt passion bolt through his heart. His treasure. He took her away at once. He moved her into a room behind the kitchen of the house wherein his ancient wife lay dying. None of his friends, or his wife, for that matter, ever suspected that Irene was his daughter. He told them all that she was the new downstairs maid. This was typical of his essential innocence. Nobody for a moment believed that Irene was a downstairs maid. Instead it was generally agreed that she was the old man's mistress. As a maid, however, Irene was wonderful to watch, and his friends found it amusing to go along with the pretense. Irene wore a little French apron over the cashmere sweaters and expensive skirts the old man had purchased for her on his wife's charge accounts. She performed her simple tasks with elaborate precision, as though to convey each nuance of meaning in pantomine to the guests who assembled every afternoon for drinks out on the terrace. She beamed with inner humor, but she never spoke a word.

The old woman died. She, too, had played the game, up to the point of death. Afterward it was disclosed that she had left everything to the children of her first marriage. Irene's father got the right to use the

house and the car for the rest of his life. This put him in a state of pan-
ic. He paid a visit to Irene's mother. He began to wonder aloud whether
it had been such a good idea after all to move Irene into the house
while his wife was still alive. Irene's mother cut him short. Marry
Irene, she said. Don't even think twice. She'll know exactly what to do.
Irene by now was going about in pearls and high-heeled shoes. She had
placed the funeral flowers in pots and set them on every available surface throughout the downstairs rooms. This scheme of Irene's mother
almost broke the old man's heart with joy. He dashed home and married Irene in a gay, flower-bedecked ceremony in the living room in the
presence of his rich friends. How bold they all thought he was to take a
ravishing bride young enough to be his daughter before his wife was
even cold in her grave. Irene they loved. She was such fun. She glowed.
She made everything in life seem like such a game. She hardly ever
spoke above a whisper. Her new friends did all the talking. They
rushed to her aid. They showed her how to write a complete menu.
They taught her how to cut a deck of cards. They taught her how to do
the cha-cha. Irene never forgot a single thing she learned. She swiftly
expanded her repertoire. Soon she was playing the lead role in a chic
romantic comedy. She and the old man kicked off the summer season
with a Bastille Day masquerade. Their friends outspent one another
lavishly to come up with original costumes to wear to this day-long
drinking revel.

The old man supported them for a time by cashing in stock certifi-
cates that various friends had given him over the years for Christmas.
When these were exhausted, Irene's mother came to the rescue. She
had continued to live down in the Salad Bowl. She advised Irene to
open a dress shop. Thanks to her mother, Irene was superbly equipped
for this undertaking. She immediately organized her new friends to invest in a shop and called it Charades. Charades became the most fashionable dress shop on the Monterey Peninsula. Irene sent her father
over to the Salinas Valley once a week with a pile of garments for her
mother to alter. The old man also drove Irene to work every day. He
drove a powder blue Lincoln Continental convertible of prewar vintage
with white sidewall tires. He played the part of the indulgent old *pa-*

tron to perfection. He used to wait for Irene outside the shop in the early evening. He affected a style of dress that might have been favored by a boulevardier in the South of France. He wore a red neckerchief, a blue smock, and a wide-brimmed straw hat with a flat crown. He always stood by while Irene settled herself comfortably in the front seat before he closed the door on her side of the car, as though he were tucking her in for the night. Irene completed the picture. She wore a brightly colored scarf to protect her hair when she rode in the open car. She could be seen chatting away to the old man like an animated high school beauty queen as they cruised slowly homeward together with the top down.

It came as no surprise when their union went the way of all May–December marriages. Sadly, but not too sadly, everyone realized that Irene was growing up. How marvelous, though, it had been while it lasted. She had made the old rascal so happy and mellow. Yet how could it have turned out any other way? Irene was now a successful businesswoman. Charades took up all her time. The shop was her salon. Here it was that her large circle of admirers gathered to gossip and chat even when Irene was not actually there, for she was often away at fashion shows. It was a life in which the old man could play a role of only peripheral importance. It was clear that Irene now merely tolerated the old man whenever he came to the shop. He hovered in the background. At dinner parties he drank too much and went to sleep at the table. How tiresome that must have been for Irene, everyone agreed. No wonder she left him to fend for himself when she traveled around the country to buy finery to sell off her racks.

One bright October day Irene flew off to Paris to attend the fall openings of the great French fashion houses. She met a billionaire in the Parc Monceau. He introduced her to his world: his house on the rue St.-Honoré, his château in the country, his racing stables in Auteuil. Irene returned briefly to get a divorce and make all the necessary arrangements. She no longer had any use for Charades. She gave the shop to her father. In the years that followed he could be seen at nightfall locking up by himself. He was said to be brokenhearted. Irene's mother never did join him. The last thing she wanted to do in life was to look after the old roustabout in his useless dotage. Someone else manages the shop and cares for him now. Irene never sees him. Her new husband forbids it. There is no room in his world for the past. Irene, however, has not neglected her mother. French fashion designers regularly send Irene their latest creations free of charge on the off chance that she will be seen wearing them in the society layouts of *Vogue* and *Harper's Bazaar,* and she always forwards the cocktail dresses on to the Salinas Valley.

A Soldier of Fortunes

Gato was Mexican. He always passed for an American, however. He spoke English in a slightly querulous monotone without a trace of a Mexican inflection. Someone told me that he had learned how to speak English from an American baby-sitter employed by his family in Mexico City when he was a child. Someone else was always filling me in about Gato. His first wife, an American madonna, told me that he had fallen madly in love with her and pursued her ceaselessly all over Mexico City, when she was an exchange student, until, against the wishes of her father, a newspaper publisher, she at last had consented to marry him. Gato forbade her afterward to see her friends and family. According to her they had lived for a long time in isolation. Gato was a correspondent based in the Rome office of an American news magazine when I first knew them. At that time they lived behind the walls of an estate on the Appian Way. I don't think they ever entertained there together. Once, when Gato was away on a story in North Africa, his wife gave a cocktail party. On that occasion she told me that he had habitually locked her up in the house in Mexico City whenever he went out, so that she couldn't escape. She was often imprisoned there for weeks at a time. She feared his jealousy, she said.

A colleague told me of Gato's exploits when he was based in Hong Kong. He was on a real merry-go-round out there. Nobody ever met his wife unless they visited his house on the Peak. Gato went to all the official cocktail parties by himself. I happened to mention to this colleague of Gato that his wife was a woman of considerable beauty. The colleague told me that he had seen our friend often in the company of beautiful women not one of whom could have been called his wife. The correspondent sort of muttered this information. They had covered the war in Indochina together.

Someone, I forget who, told me how Gato lost his job. It may not have been one single person. I probably put the story together from things that several people told me. Gato had a weakness for women, exclusively rich ones as I came to discover, and while supposedly on assignment in places like Laos, he was really on assignations in places like Bali. He'd assemble his story from newsclips when he got back to Hong Kong. He also relied on stringers to cable him eyewitness material from the trouble spot about which he was reporting. In some instances he invented his own colorful copy. He was fired for writing a story about Sumatra that was discovered to be the exact copy, names and dates changed, of one that he had written some years earlier about Cyprus.

I saw Gato once again in Mexico City. He was no longer a journalist. He was now working for the family construction business. Someone else said that it was actually an undertaking firm. Gato was coming out of a nightclub in the Zona Rosa at the time of our first encounter late one hot summer night. He and his wife were living in another part of town. He gave me his telephone number. I called him later to ask him for a loan. We met on a street corner where he handed me a thick roll of one-hundred-dollar bills, an outstanding gesture of natural generosity on his part. Somewhat to the embarrassment of us both we encountered each other soon afterward on the back street of a fishing village on the Gulf coast. He was in the company of a woman who was not his wife and whom I would not hesitate to describe as exciting. We dined together. A dog sauntered over to our table and tipped his dinner into his lap with its nose. "I guess this just isn't my night," remarked Gato to his companion with good-natured rue.

Gato's wife left him and went back to the States with their children to live with her parents. Quite unexpectedly I got this story from a girl in Litchfield County who had known Gato during the last year or so of his marriage. This girl was quite rich. He had fallen madly in love with her, but she had resisted him, although with great difficulty, I gathered, because he had pursued her with a frenzied single-mindedness. She was not the only American postdebutante in whom Gato had expressed an interest. She said that his behavior had become the talk of Mexico City. His wife had walked out on a big private banquet in Cuernavaca to protest his behavior on the dance floor. Some time after his wife left him he, too, showed up in the States, although not to reconcile with his wife, who by now had divorced him. He was in San Antonio for a time, the widow of an old China hand told me, to research a screenplay he planned to write for a docudrama about illegal aliens.

The girl in Litchfield County kept me up-to-date. Gato married a woman who lived in Hartford. She was the only child of an aviation-equipment manufacturer. She was a divorcée with a couple of kids. She had a few million bucks. Gato moved into her comfortable house. He took the kids to school. They led a reclusive life on her money. They rarely left the house. They did all their shopping over the telephone. Gato persuaded her to build a movie theater and they ordered the movies they wanted to see and held select private screenings. Guests were invited to watch movies while having after-dinner drinks. They bought a winter place on a secluded bay in Costa Rica, where they were waited on by servants. Gato's wife grew heavyset in the course of the marriage, according to my Litchfield County informant.

One day an item about him appeared in a nationally syndicated gossip column. According to the gossip columnist Gato was now the proprietor of a magazine for wine connoisseurs. He was living in Palm Beach. He had created a stir there by eloping with the daughter of a German steel magnate. He had broken up her marriage to a French nobleman, a vintner. The girl from Litchfield County was reluctant to discuss the matter, but I understood from her that he had gone through all his second wife's money and then left her watching reruns of old movies in Hartford. How Gato got from Hartford to Palm Beach is a mystery. He must have staked himself to the wine magazine on the last of his wife's money and then obtained entry to the nobleman's château on the basis of his credentials as a connoisseur of wines, although I'm just imagining all this. Then, upon falling madly in love with the princess, he must have pursued her relentlessly until she agreed to elope. She got a quick Haitian divorce and, if accounts in the gossip columns may be trusted, they tied the knot in Rio de Janeiro. Gato has finally outgrown the American baby-sitter. The newlyweds now divide their time between a house the princess owns in Palm Beach, called the Villa Today, and her Monte Carlo residence, the Villa Aujord'hui.

Settembrino's Mother

She had been at one time in her youth a Spanish dancer. She was now married to Prince Borodin. Previously she had been married to the duke of Otranto. Her current lover and future husband was an American dynast named Howland Blaine. The prince, the princess, and Howland Blaine went about together. They used to arrive together before the entrance of our private school every afternoon at three o'clock to pick up Settembrino. The prince drove them in his black Jaguar sedan, which he handled as though he were in the Milia Miglia. Princess Borodin usually sat in back. Howland Blaine was crammed into the front seat with his shoulder pressed against the window. On days when Settembrino's team played a soccer match, the princess, the prince, and Howland Blaine could be found standing together on the sidelines. Howland Blaine stood behind the prince and princess and watched the soccer game over their heads. Sometimes they could be seen walking together on the outskirts of town.

The prince, the princess, and Howland Blaine also visited other people's houses together. Howland Blaine was the center of attraction on these occasions. He was a huge, gregarious man who naturally dominated the room. He was offered the most comfortable armchair when they came to our house. The prince sat in a straight-backed chair beside the one in which Howland Blaine had settled. The princess, from wherever she happened to be, called upon Howland Blaine to tell everyone what he thought about a given topic under discussion because the scope of his knowledge and intelligence and acquaintance was so much greater than that of anyone else present, and the prince would sit forward, elbows on knees, cigarette burning between the fingers of his clenched hands, head down, and look out at the room with a worried expression on his face while Howland Blaine expounded in a genial, booming voice on jai alai, British relations with the Vatican after World War II, the tennis game of Henri Cochet, the latest aircraft technology, movie colony chitchat, the medicinal uses of curare, Endicott Peabody, the growth of Western influence on Chinese painting in the seventeenth century, or the strategy of Settembrino's soccer coach. It did not matter to him. He had an enormous appetite for talk. The princess made herself comfortable wherever she was. She had such a limber dancer's body that she could contort herself with ease or perch on surfaces most people would find unbearably hard after a short time. She sometimes lay on the floor with her head propped against a chair across the living room from Howland Blaine and stared straight in front of her while Howland Blaine talked. Or else she ended up lying on our couch with the well-formed calf of one trousered leg crossed over the upraised knee of the other but situated in such a way that she rested her back against the corner of the couch and faced Howland Blaine. She would sit on the floor sometimes for a whole hour, arms hugging her knees, while Howland Blaine discoursed, and grin sideways at our mother, and say, "Isn't it the most absolutely fascinating thing in the world?" She always wore slacks, embroidered velvet slippers, a little blue velvet blazer, and a necklace made of emeralds, rubies, and pearls.

Our nurse despised the princess. She was a ruthless moral judge who was never swayed by mitigating claims of any kind. She ruled our household. She was often invited to join the guests for cocktails, where she could make her intensely felt opinions clear to everyone, but when the prince and princess showed up with Howland Blaine she chose not to come forth. She said that the princess was the scum of the earth. "She's a born slut," she used to say, "and he's no better than she is, that little runt of a husband, eh? He certainly likes to keep his tail between his legs, though, doesn't he?" She'd laugh, because the image of a whipped dog that the prince had inspired was in her opinion so richly what he deserved. She stayed in her cave behind the kitchen when they came to visit, although she did maintain an entirely personal, private relationship with Howland Blaine, who always went back there to pay a call on her before he departed. They jawboned out in the laundry room in front of her cave for ten or fifteen minutes. At such times our nurse could release a curveball of charm. She was a hefty woman who wore thick-heeled pumps. She wore elastic garter belts to strap in her unruly flesh. She had, even in that sun-blessed climate, a complexion the color of the oatmeal cereal she used to serve us every morning for breakfast. She had a big beaked nose, plentiful jowls that shook when she was enraged, shrewd eyes, and fine hair of a light, tarnished red color. She abhorred rich people. Howland Blaine must somehow have thought it was necessary to touch base with her, unable, perhaps, to resist the scent of challenge to his skill as a diplomat. He hulked over our nurse with a big white smile while they talked about the horses. Our nurse bet on the horses; Howland Blaine, although he did not own any horses, had always been a big shot in racing circles. They gabbed together about Willie Shoemaker and Native Dancer while Prince and Princess Borodin cooled their heels out in the front hall. Our nurse enjoyed it when the high and the mighty, as she put it, paid their respects to her. She was glad to see Howland Blaine. "Isn't he a great one," she used to say. "But don't ever ask me what he sees in that scarlet woman because I wouldn't be able to tell you."

The prince and princess lived in a large white villa at the top of an emerald-green lawn. You could see their house from the bottom of their driveway through a screen of live oaks that spread their branches over the lower slopes of the lawn. We were invited there once for Settembrino's ninth birthday party. The downstairs rooms were airy and bright. Windows on both sides of the living room let in the daylight. The floors were covered with oriental carpets. An enormous tapestry hung from the ceiling at the far end of the room. The furniture was a comfortable mix of English modern and extremely good Italian antiques. A select group of European parents sat around in the living room, while the children as they arrived were politiely introduced and then led offstage by Settembrino's nurse to another part of the house, where we were treated to pancakes. Each child received a gift from Settembrino in exchange for the one given to him. I recall going through the living room later on an errand. It was empty, and curtains billowed gently at the sides of French windows, which were open onto the back lawn. We played hide-and-seek. Settembrino was a merry, fun-loving boy. He was an exuberant although badly disciplined boy, by our standards. He was not allowed to play at our house. Yet he was not ill tempered, merely spoiled. He was forced to wear the clothes that an upper-class European boy would wear to school or a party. He wore knee socks, gray woolen shorts, a blue cashmere V-neck sweater, a white shirt, and a necktie. In this attire he naturally looked unkempt in a short time. During the game of hide-and-seek he beckoned me out of doors. He motioned to me, finger on lips, to remain silent. He led me down a garden path through the oak trees in the back of the house to a steep hillside covered with ivy and then crawled on his bare knees through the undergrowth until we reached the edge of a ravine. There, the hill fell away into the deep canyon below, where a thin trickle threaded between sun-dazzled boulders in a parched creekbed. The adults I had last seen in the living room were down in the canyon disporting themselves on the littoral. Clothes were scattered about at the foot of the embankment. Prince Borodin in the lower left-hand corner appeared to be wrestling with the naked wife of the Scandinavian orthopedist in the shade of an overhanging oak. The composition, the light, drew my attention upstream. Howland Blaine, in the full blare of the sun, lay back on his elbows in the gravel while the princess rode him. Howland Blaine was whiter than white. The princess was entirely brown. Settembrino and I watched with eager entrancement. You can see us. We're the winged cupids in the upper left-hand corner of the painting.

Mr. and Mrs. Noonan

Mr. and Mrs. Noonan lived in a Monterey-style house situated on a slight rise from which they could look out upon the Pacific Ocean. To reach their house from the road you ascended a short paved incline at the rear of their property that ended at the border of a lawn, where a brick walkway led straight across the grass courtyard to a row of French doors, through which you could glimpse the Pacific framed by windows across the open downstairs rooms. Sometimes you were admitted by a maid fitted out in a black satin uniform edged at the collar and cuffs with white lace trim who ushered you over gray wall-to-wall carpeting to a book-lined library or, when the weather was warm, to the terrace beyond, where the air was perfumed by the exudations of Korean moss, a carpet of green fur that appeared to underlie the terrace and the juniper landscape of the hillside and thickly enfolded the stepping-stones of a footpath that wound down around the hillside within the deep shade of cypress to a private beach enclosure below. Sometimes you were greeted at the door by Mr. Noonan himself.

Mr. Noonan was a bantam-size man, slightly bowlegged, who wore his white hair sleekly combed. He wore horn-rimmed glasses with thick lenses. On occasion he wore a shirt with a turtleneck collar. More often he wore a white shirt, a necktie, a tweed jacket, and dark gray slacks. He seated you in comfort on a couch and sat slightly sideways at one end of the couch to face you or on the edge of a chair he had drawn up close to the couch to be near you. He adjusted his trousers at the knees after he sat down. He leaned forward, hands folded, head down, and listened intently to what you had to say. Mr. Noonan had an appetite for good talk. He liked clarity. His own speech was richly exclamatory, and he frequently punched the fist of one hand into the palm of his other for emphasis. Mr. Noonan's speech still bore the traces of a Missouri accent. He had a fleshy nose and hyperactive salivary glands, and he often blew his nose quickly with a pocket handkerchief and was known to accompany his expletives with a shower of saliva. Sometimes he cackled and exhibited his large shiny tongue, which lay in his mouth like a pink oyster. When the maid appeared in the doorway Mr. Noonan sprang to his feet. He did not like to draw the maid into the foreground. He asked you what you wanted to drink and gave her instructions in the back of the room and then dismissed her.

For many years Mr. Noonan had kept himself successfully occupied investing his wife's fortune and reading up on post-Industrial Revolution politics of the West, not excluding those of the Soviet Union. He was almost, but not quite, a Communist. He was convinced that capital could be redistributed according to the theory set forth by Marx and Engels, although he believed that the Soviet experiment had been led astray by Uncle Joe Stalin, as he called him, but at heart he was a socialist and a critic of laissez-faire capitalism. He was a student of Max Weber and Thorstein Veblen and Sydney Webb, but he identified himself with George Bernard Shaw, and like Shaw, he was a lapsed Catholic of Irish descent who railed against the propagation of religion, which he called pie in the sky. He thought Harry S Truman was a son of a bitch. He regretted that William O. Douglas had not been selected in 1944 to run for vice-president on the Democratic ticket with Franklin D. Roosevelt and believed that he would have been chosen had it not been for a certain rigged telephone call. In 1948 he voted for Henry Wallace. He thought George F. Kennan was a good man and he quite liked Adlai E. Stevenson, but he might have had some reservations about the sons of Joseph P. Kennedy, even though they had all gone to Harvard. Mr. Noonan was proud of his Harvard education. He was a contemporary at Harvard of Walter Lippmann and Heywood Broun and Robert Benchley. He had seen something of Bob Benchley, as he called him, during the 1930s when Benchley lived in Hollywood. Mr. Noonan had once upon a time kept company with a rich assortment of sporting people for whom Hollywood had been a favored playground, though he had long since turned violently against some of this cohort for political reasons.

Guests were well into their second drink by the time Mrs. Noonan drifted into the library. She was taller than Mr. Noonan. Sometimes she wore slacks, a blouse, and an unbuttoned sweater. Often, however, she wore a floor-length bathrobe and straw slippers. Mrs. Noonan gave the impression that she was permanently convalescent. She had used a variety of afflictions, youthful tuberculosis and chronic allergies, to influence the course of her married life, which she had financed largely with her own Saint Louis liquor distillery inheritance, into exclusively temperate climes. Her *Dame aux Camélias* appearance enhanced the tone of pathos she brought to her forceful rhetoric. She addressed her guests from a standing position with an emotional intensity that whitened the skin around her flared, pointed nostrils. She was no longer beautiful and perhaps she had never been. Her set of prominent, though not excessively buck, upper teeth would have denied her the perfection of beauty, but she was elegant. She had a distinguished facial bone structure and her efforts to erase any evidence of advancing age had met with some success. Her skin was almost without wrinkles. She was slender, like a young girl. She washed her shoulder-length hair a honey-brown hue and banged it above her brow. She never exposed her skin to direct sunlight because her pigment manufactured freckles under the sun's transforming rays. Down at their private beach enclosure, where the Noonans maintained a whitewashed cabana made of smooth round rocks cemented together and covered with a corrugated roof, Mrs. Noonan wore a white terrycloth robe and carried an open parasol on her shoulder as she stood in the hot sand and declaimed her heartfelt stories in an urgent, contralto delivery, which she punctuated now and again with deep chuckles.

She was not interested in politics. She was a storyteller. She had the talent to put stories about people she knew into dramatic narrative. She could exalt the most unsavory social malefactor by the force of her pathos. Her subversive chuckle was the price she exacted for this service. None of her stories met with Mr. Noonan's complete approval. He liked intelligent conversation with people of either sex, especially sexually attractive women, the younger and smarter the better. He was not carried away by what he would have called bathos. He, like Mrs. Noonan, was grieved by the misfortune of friends; he was otherwise unmoved by stories about people who had brought catastrophe upon themselves foolishly. In the presence of guests he often took issue with how Mrs. Noonan reported the facts. He insisted on getting the facts straight. His wife objected even more vehemently, in the presence of guests, to Mr. Noonan's objections. Sometimes they vociferated loudly at the same time like opera singers performing separate but concurrent recitative.

Mr. and Mrs. Noonan had traveled to the French Riviera in the late twenties and early thirties. For Mrs. Noonan it must have been the zenith of her life. She had lived on the Continent as a child. She used to lament the introduction to Paris of the automobile because she could recall how in a more restful time she had traveled by horse-drawn cab along the snow-carpeted Champs-Elysées on winter evenings. After not a few transatlantic crossings Mr. Noonan refused to budge. Mrs. Noonan grew restless. Soon she fell in love with a man-about-town who shall be known as Fremont. She asked Mr. Noonan for a divorce so that she could marry Fremont. Mr. Noonan blew his top. He refused under any circumstances to agree to a divorce. Mrs. Noonan fled to Europe with Fremont. She traveled extensively on the Continent with Fremont for two or three years while Mr. Noonan bided his time at home. War broke out soon enough just as Mr. Noonan surely must have known it would. He fired off a cable to Mrs. Noonan: TIME TO COME HOME. Home she came. Fremont in later years could be seen pushing a shopping cart through a local grocery store with the woman, not Mrs. Noonan, whom he had eventually married.

Mr. and Mrs. Noonan had no children. They counted children among their friends, however. They talked to children with the same enthusiasm they brought to conversation with adults. They never talked down to children. Mr. Noonan liked to talk to the young about the variety of capitalist ills and the New Deal and the McCarthy era and the presidential follies of Dwight D. Eisenhower, among other subjects. Mrs. Noonan told true stories to children about people she knew. Mr. and Mrs. Noonan never differentiated between their guests. Their lunch parties and dinners were attended by café society nobs, local blue bloods, intellectual liberals, and people under the age of eighteen. Though they lavished refreshments on their guests, later in life Mr. and Mrs. Noonan were abstemious in most ways. Mr. Noonan had stopped smoking cigarettes in his early sixties. He had also stopped taking caffeine, although his Oldsmobile sedan could be seen parked outside a pharmacy about a mile and a half from his house in the morning hours while he was inside sneaking a few quick cups of coffee. The Noonans no longer drank alcoholic beverages, although the exquisite meals prepared by their French cook for dinner parties were accompanied by the best French wines and champagne. Mr. and Mrs. Noonan upended their wineglasses when they sat down at the table, and in his last years Mr. Noonan also turned his dinner plate upside down before the maid came around with the food.

Mr. Noonan's language, however, had grown commensurably libidinous and profane. At the end of his life Mr. Noonan spiced his strongly held views with colloquial references to the male anatomy. Perhaps his reading had affected his speech. He was an avid fan in later life of European erotic novels. He was known to urge these books on much younger women of his acquaintance for reading and discussion. Mr. Noonan's salty language also began to flavor Mrs. Noonan's storytelling, which became more explicitly scandalous as time went by, although no less theatrical. She used Mr. Noonan's own vivid vocabulary to add her support to his by now inflammatory Marxist opinions.

Mrs. Noonan was away visiting relatives when Mr. Noonan, who was not yet eighty years old, developed a tumor in his brain. In a matter of days he began to lose his memory. He was aware of what was happening but he failed to inform Mrs. Noonan, who undoubtedly would have flown home to be at his side. Instead, he wrote notes to himself and placed them throughout the house to remind him of things that he knew he might forget. He also left messages for Mrs. Noonan, which she found upon her return. She was summoned home by the maid after Mr. Noonan had been taken, unconscious, to the hospital. Mr. Noonan never regained consciousness. His robust body refused to give up easily, however, and he lived on for many months, tossing ceaselessly in his hospital bed, locked in a wrestling match with death. Mrs. Noonan survived him by a few years, fretful but ever more forgetful, until she, too, faded out of the picture.

Circe

Mary Louise Calhoun was a Charleston belle. Her husband, Willie Calhoun, had been an architecture student at the time of their marriage, although later he quit school to become a real estate dealer. He had a bloodless southern pallor and short reddish-brown hair, which he parted in the middle. Mary Louise Calhoun adored him. You could see why. He had the face of a slightly spoiled cherub. He was solid, confident, and spoke in slow Carolina drawl. He and Mary Louise had fallen madly in love at the age of eighteen. He made Mary Louise happy. She looked like someone who is dreaming. She had wide, high cheekbones and a full, slow smile and elongated, slitted eyes. She had a proud face. She wore her silky hair around her shoulders and had what appeared to be a haughty mannerism of tossing her hair when it fell loosely around her face. She may have been bored with Willie Calhoun without knowing it. He was a protégé of her father. After the architecture school decision, as it was always called, her father had purchased for Willie a junior partnership in a Charleston real estate firm. Mary Louise gamely accompanied Willie on business dinners to various Charleston fish restaurants, where she was compelled to make conversation with her husband's prospective clients over the she-crab soup. This did not interest her greatly, but she still deeply loved Willie Calhoun. She was able to put up with the sound of his voice droning on about commercial properties and resort developments by slipping off to the ladies' room between courses or sipping discreetly away at her wine. She was always dreaming. She enjoyed her life with Willie. They had no children. They lived in a house on King Street.

Willie Calhoun was always trying to persuade Uncle Stephen to sell some of his land so that his firm could develop it. He and Mary Louise often went down to stay with her uncle at Wildwood Hall. At night, after dinner, they would play backgammon by the fire. Willie Calhoun liked to assume the role of real estate baron when they played backgammon. Mary Louise found this affectation appealing at first. Willie wore a white vest and smoked a long Havana cigar from Uncle Stephen's moldering supply while he drank Uncle Stephen's five-star brandy and condescended to him about real estate values. Uncle Stephen was amused by the boy's presumption. He was a gentle, but stubborn, bachelor. His house reflected it. The rooms smelled strongly of mildew. The paint was flaking off the ceilings. Water stains had discolored the wallpaper in the downstairs rooms. The pillars that upheld the portico were rotting. The family portraits that hung on the dining room walls were badly in need of cleaning and restoration. None of this bothered Uncle Stephen. He, too, lived in a dream. He liked to dream about the life he might have led had he not retired at an early age to breed field dogs on his inherited land. He lived in genteel poverty and barely managed to pay his estate taxes, although his land was worth a fortune, and if he had been willing to sell even a fraction of the estate and invest the proceeds he could have paid his taxes with the interest. So Willie Calhoun often told him.

Uncle Stephen dropped dead of a heart attack one afternoon during dog trials at Wildwood Hall. The plantation was put up for sale. Willie got into the act at once. He was excited. His real estate firm was among those that listed the property. He was on the inside track. If he could sell the property he would also very likely be made a full partner. Mary Louise could not share his excitement. Wildwood Hall was part of her dream. It was the playground of her imagination. She had never envisioned a future without it. Willie seemed oblivious to her feelings. He drove her down to Wildwood Hall for a last weekend before the movers came to take away the furniture. The following Monday a prospective buyer was coming and Willie had arranged the visit so that he and Mary Louise could show him around together. Willie conducted Mary Louise on a practice tour through the house and pointed out to her all the architectural features that could be used to advantage if someone bought Wildwood Hall and turned it into a center for design research or an arts community. He was expansive. It rained the whole weekend and much of the time he spent making love to Mary Louise in Uncle Stephen's big double bed. He was just as excited by Mary Louise as he had been when they first made love, as teenagers, out at Folly Beach. She had widely spaced, rounded breasts and a stormy sexual energy when aroused. She was a prize. He told Mary Louise that with part of his agent's commission from the sale he would buy her a boat.

The prospective buyer was a millionaire from Birmingham named

Piggy Greenway. He was called Piggy because he looked and always had looked porcine. It was a childhood nickname. He was short, plump, had an upturned nose that looked like an electrical outlet of some kind, and a pink face set in a smooth layer of fat. He was silver haired. He was in his fifties. Mary Louise came out to greet him on the veranda wearing jodhpurs, old duck hunting boots, a black velvet riding jacket, and a black velvet ribbon in her long chestnut hair. Piggy fell in love with her immediately. To him she must have looked like the image of aristocratic southern pulchritude in her mourning habit. He told Mary Louise that he wanted to buy the place if he could buy her, too. Willie heard him. He walked behind them. He was amused and gratified by the spectacle of the plump little millionaire hurrying to keep up with his wife as she strode across the fields. He keeps *touching* me, she complained to Willie when they were alone for a few minutes back at the house. Let him, Willie said. You are doing *great*. Just do your thing, he told her. She looked at herself in the downstairs hallway mirror. What is *my* thing? she wondered. She applied a touch of lipstick. This added a little zest to her mourning ensemble. They all drove back to Charleston. That was how Piggy did things. He decided on the spur of the moment to go somewhere else, and everyone piled into automobiles and took off. To Mary Louise this was exciting. It banished the gloom of Uncle Stephen's death. She sat with Piggy in the back seat of his rented limousine. Willie drove with Piggy's secretary in their car. Piggy Greenway told Mary Louise right away that he wanted to marry her. He was subdued and well behaved in the back seat of the rented limousine. Oh but Mr. Greenway don't be silly, she told him. Too silly. How old *are* you anyway? No really don't be a silly fool. I mean be a silly fool by all means of course, you must, *are* a silly fool but I *am* married, I do have a husband and he *is* possessive. Really. I mean it. I mean honestly. She entertained him and herself all the way back to town in the rain with this badinage and then they all went to a fish restaurant for dinner. Piggy drank Jack Daniels on the rocks. Willie drank scotch. I truly love your wife, Piggy Greenway told Willie Calhoun over dinner. Maybe we can work something out. Oh don't be silly, said Mary Louise. I'm just as serious as I can be, replied Piggy Greenway.

He's *not* serious, Mary Louise announced the next day, when she and Willie awoke with hangovers. Willie couldn't be certain. He was too hung over. He was not distressed, however, when Piggy Greenway sent two dozen yellow roses to Mary Louise before he departed for Birmingham. Piggy was going to return the following weekend. He was going to seriously consider a real estate development scheme that Willie had proposed. The Birmingham financier was interested. He called Mary Louise at home during the week from Birmingham to tell her that he still loved her and wanted to marry her. That was all he cared about. He would give her anything she wanted. This churned her up. She told Willie about it when he came home that night. He was delighted. Look, it's *great* that Mr. Greenway has fallen in love with you, he said. He is serious, she said. Do you understand? He really means it. Well, that's ridiculous, said Willie. He laughed. It's true, she retorted. He proposed to me today on the telephone and he proposed to me on Monday in his car. Well, don't spurn him yet, for Christ's sake, Willie said. Give me some more time. String him along.

Friday came real fast, as Uncle Stephen used to say. Mary Louise was dreading it. She was unable to concentrate on anything. She was marking time until the telephone rang late Friday night. She picked up the receiver with a beating heart. It was Piggy. He'd been delayed, he said, by bad weather. Now, even though it was late, he wanted to invite them for dinner. Willie and Mary Louise had already eaten but they joined him anyway. Mary Louise nursed a scotch while the men ate. Willie had a second dinner of oysters, baked crab in Mornay sauce, and a hazelnut torte. After dinner they drank brandy. The weekend went by in a whirl. Piggy gave them a wonderful time. They went everywhere in his limousine. They never stopped drinking. Piggy had a stocked bar in the back seat. Mary Louise was in control the entire time. Power made her euphoric. She kept looking at Willie Calhoun, wondering if he'd stop her, or reprimand her. It was so obvious that she was getting Piggy ever more deeply involved. Willie told her she was doing great. Just keep it up, he told her. Oh stop saying that, she wanted to tell him, but she merely smiled. She felt slightly ill. On Sunday night, on the way home, she told him that Piggy had invited her for breakfast the next morning in his hotel suite. Do you mind? She asked him. Good Christ no, Willie said. You can defend yourself. He's got something up his sleeve he hasn't told me about. Maybe you can find out what it is. All I know is that if he waits too much longer some other smart-ass billionaire is going to gobble up that property.

She wore a ribbon in her hair. She wore slacks and low-heeled pumps and a blue cashmere sweater. Piggy bounced around his hotel suite in a white silk dressing gown, which he wore over his shirt and trousers. He ordered champagne. Mary Louise seated herself in a comfortable wing chair with her purse in her lap. She felt like someone in love. She was at a high pitch of sexual excitement. They talked small talk, as two people urgently in love do, to stave off the inevitable rush of passion. The champagne arrived. Piggy asked the waiter to uncork it, which he did. He poured two glasses. Piggy dismissed him. Piggy got up from the sofa and carried a glass of champagne around to her. She sipped it and put her glass on the table beside her. What's it to be? Piggy asked her. He stood beside her. Will you marry me? She tossed her mane. If, and when, you accept Willie's price, she said. What is it? Piggy wanted to know. Two million, she said. In cash. Hot diggety-dog it's a deal, cried Piggy Greenway. Plus until we tie the knot I don't want you to touch me, understand? That's how we Charleston girls like to do business. You can sniff but that's it, okay? He looked chastened. We'd better get something in writing, he said. Just take my word for it, said Mary Louise. She felt shaky, but her voice was calm, final sounding. Scout's honor? he inquired. Cross my heart and hope to die, said Mary Louise Calhoun. She turned her widely spaced, rounded breasts in his direction. And one more thing, Mr. Greenway: Would you kindly put me in charge of the disposition of the land? Do it with a rider or something. Piggy's face turned deep red. I intend to give you the house and property outright, he said, for a wedding present.

Lunch was subdued but festive. As they sat there after toasting each other with champagne cocktails Willie, flushed with triumph, said to Mary Louise, I don't know what you did but it sure did work. I just did *my* thing, said Mary Louise brightly. Piggy held his tongue. He made a down payment on Wildwood Hall in the living room of his hotel suite after lunch over coffee and brandy. Willie, at Piggy's suggestion, agreed to split the commission with Mary Louise. Soon spring was in the air. Mary Louise and Willie Calhoun began going down to Wildwood Hall as guests of Piggy Greenway. Piggy turned the job of restoring the house over to Mary Louise. She told him to put her on the payroll, which he did. She then told Willie that she was Piggy's consultant. Now Willie was euphoric. Mary Louise was self-possessed. She still looked like a crafty dreamer. Now, when they went down to Wildwood Hall, she was in charge. Piggy had lost none of his ardor for Mary Louise, his prospective bride. In the springtime he was more in love with her than ever. He followed her all around the house while she told him what she planned to do. Upstairs, in the master bedroom, where she now slept with Willie Calhoun as Piggy's guest, she talked about *our* bedroom and *our* upstairs living room. Piggy listened obediently, hands folded behind him on his rump, cocking his head pertly this way and that while Mary Louise, in riding habit, spoke in practical terms about ceiling repairs, roofing, moldings, all the things that had to be done. Sure thing, he'd say. Money was no object. She had a budget of half a million dollars. She wanted to rebuild the stables and repair the greenhouse. All this Piggy promised to do. He brought his own hunting dogs over from Alabama and took them out on field exercises with Mary Louise. He never asked her how she intended to deal with Willie Calhoun. He never troubled her with talk of that kind. He had complete confidence in Mary Louise. She knew that. They worked well together.

Willie played golf on Saturdays and came down to Wildwood Hall late Saturday afternoon. On Sunday he nursed a hangover out on the veranda, where Piggy's majordomo served him bacon, eggs, sausage, toast, grits, orange juice, applesauce, and café au lait. Willie enjoyed himself. He was just now beginning to feel rich. Piggy had agreed to pay two million dollars, about three quarters of a million more than the asking price, which would make Willie richer by about two hundred thousand dollars. So far he had received one third of that amount. According to the schedule of financing that Piggy had arranged through his corporate trust, the money would be all paid up by December 31. He liked to sit out on the veranda and daydream about his new wealth while Mary Louise and Piggy worked out with the dogs in the lower fields. It was quite like the old days with Uncle Stephen, only much better. The pillars had been replaced, the veranda repainted. Wildwood Hall was no longer gloomy. He liked to compliment Mary Louise on what a fine job she had done to land the Flying Pig, which was a new sobriquet he had bestowed upon Piggy, who often flew his own jet over to Wildwood Hall from Birmingham. He was amused by Piggy. They played backgammon and drank, while Willie acted the role of real estate baron just as he once had done with Uncle Stephen, giving Piggy advice about Charleston development schemes. Mary Louise played backgammon with businesslike detachment. She ignored him. He got drunk while they played. Piggy drank easily as much as Willie but did not get so very drunk. He usually cleaned up at backgammon, although Mary Louise did not do badly either. Piggy, who had been a flyer in World War II, liked to tell stories about his experiences in whorehouses. He was always very explicit. Willie roared with laughter. No, Willie would say the next morning as he plopped the contents of one of Piggy's miniature bottles of Jack Daniels into his morning coffee, I really like the Flying Pig. He's just so horny. And piggy.

Willie had a big belly now. He could barely squeeze into his white suit. He sweated in the hot summer sun. One Sunday in August he woke up to find himself slumped in a couch in the airy new downstairs drawing room. Piggy and Mary Louise were sitting across from him. Mary Louise wore her hair in a chignon. She was dressed in high-heeled boots and a long skirt that buttoned all the way down the front and a high-necked blouse trimmed with lace. She looked like an old-fashioned equestrienne. He heard her say that she and Piggy were leaving at noon on the first leg of a combination honeymoon and business trip to Europe. First of all they were going to fly to Alabama so that she could divorce him and marry Piggy. You need help, she said. He was sure it was true. He was too depressed to speak. He certainly could have used a drink. Perhaps, after all, none of it was of any great importance. Was he not now very rich? Piggy sat directly opposite in a navy-blue blazer, gray slacks, a yellow ascot. Mary Louise continued to address him. She gave him the name of a psychiatrist in Savannah whom her mother had used. She told him that he was probably an alcoholic. His real estate job would be up for grabs, she said, unless he pulled himself together, and he wasn't all that rich because she had legal claim to one half of the commission for the sale of Wildwood Hall. Documents to that effect, which he had signed months ago back in the living room of Piggy's hotel suite, rested securely on her lap in a folder. That left him with seventy thousand after taxes, which was about what he owed her father for setting him up in business in the first place. Piggy Greenway gazed over his bifocals at Willie Calhoun. He had a mild-mannered smile and round, baby blue eyes. We'll be gone three or four months, he said. You all may have the run of the place. Feel free. Just don't forget to let Elberta know at breakfast what you want to eat for dinner. Piggy's majordomo came in from the hallway to announce that the station wagon was waiting outside to take them to the airport. Mary Louise came around and kissed him good-bye on the lips.

Author's Note

About H. Bradfield Marquand not a very great deal is known. He seems to have been everywhere and his acquaintance is vast, yet he appears not to have been conspicuous. His life began in lavish circumstances in Pelham Manor, New York. Marquand, it is understood, did not attend any college or university. He was graced with a small trust fund at an early age and for some years, intermittently, he was employed as a steward by the Holland America Line. First-class passengers on the *Nieuw Amsterdam* were often put out after a transatlantic crossing to find Marquand dining a table or two away from them at Prunier in London on *homard flambé du vieux moine*. He was always pleasant and chatty. During the late 1960s he drove a delivery van for a garden nursery on the Monterey Peninsula that specialized in bonsai trees. He still makes a pilgrimage to Mexico in the wintertime to visit the cities of Guadalajara and Cuernavaca, where he spent so much of his childhood. He is the founding member of a drinking association known as the Kowloon Darts. Marquand has no fixed residence. The H stands for Hazzard.

About the Authors

PETER RAND is the author of two novels, *Firestorm* and *The Time of the Emergency*. He lives in New York City, where he is a Lecturer in English at Columbia University.

ELIZABETH BIRD has been a free-lance photo researcher and editor for fifteen years. She has worked for several New York City publishing houses.

Acknowledgments

For their individual help, I would like to thank: John C. Anderson, David Horvath, and Barbara Crawford and the staff of the Photographic Archives of the University of Louisville; Robin McElheny and Elizabeth Shenton at the Schlesinger Library, Radcliffe College for their time and assistance, and Jean Richardson at the Rhode Island Collection, Providence Public Library. Thanks also to the helpful staff of Prints and Photographs at the Library of Congress. My appreciation to Caroline Kozu, Gloria Withers, and Bettye Elison at the Los Angeles Public Library for their assistance with the Security Pacific National Bank Photograph collection. I am also grateful to Karyn Feiden and Deborah Waxberg at Crown and especially Dennis Lo for his enthusiasm and advice.

—E. B.

Photo Credits

The photographs in this book are from:

The Photographic Archives of the University of Louisville: The Caufield and Shook Collection, Griswold Collection, Kate Mathews Collection, Bradley Studio Collection, J. C. Rieger Collection, Vida Hunt Francis Collection, Potter Collection, Standard Oil of New Jersey Collection, and Marshall Album; The Library of Congress, Prints and Photograph Division; The American Museum of Natural History; Museum of the City of New York: The Byron Collection; Bettmann/UPI; The Schlesinger Library, Radcliffe College; Indiana State Library, Indianapolis; Providence Public Library; Pasadena Historical Society; Santa Barbara Historical Society; Security Pacific National Bank Photograph Collection/Los Angeles Public Library; University of California Los Angeles Library; California Historical Society/Title Insurance and Trust Co. (Los Angeles); Private Collections.